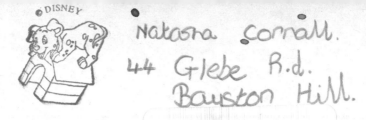

©DISNEY

Natasha Cornall.
44 Glebe Rd.
Bawston Hill.

D0581096

As the tailboard w: see Freckles, looking very small, boxed in at the far end of the truck. He whinnied and she called back to him.

"Can I lead him down?" She was dancing with excitement. "Please let me lead him down."

"Better let me do it," advised Mr Riley, spreading straw on the tailboard. "You don't want him to slip."

She watched, hardly daring to breathe, as Mr Riley led Freckles slowly down the ramp.

At last, there he was. Standing in her very own yard; her very own pony.

EMMA AND FRECKLES

Valerie Beales

Illustrated by Mary Lonsdale

MACDONALD YOUNG BOOKS

Text copyright © 1990 Valerie Beales
Illustrations copyright © 1990 May Lonsdale

First published in Great Britain in 1990
Simon & Schuster Young Books

Reprinted 1992, 1993

Reprinted in 1995 by
Macdonald Young Books Ltd
Campus 400
Maylands Avenue
Hemel Hempsted HP2 7EZ

All characters in this publication are fictitious, and any resemblance
to real persons, living or dead, is purely coincidental.

All rights reserved.

This book is sold subject to the condition that it shall not, by way of
trade or otherwise, be lent, re-sold, hired out, or otherwise circulated
without the publisher's prior consent in any form of binding or
cover other than that in which it is published and without a similar
condition including this condition being imposed on the subsequent
purchaser.

Photoset in North Wales by
Derek Doyle & Associates, Mold, Clwyd
Printed and bound in Great Britain at
The Guernsey Press

British Library Cataloguing in Publication Data

Beales, Valerie
  Emma and Freckles
  I. Title
  823'.914 [J]

ISBN 0 7500 0263 8
ISBN 0 7500 0264 6 Pbk

*To my husband, Philip,
and children, David, Martin,
Julia and Sylvia, and to
all animals, everywhere.*

Chapter One

Emma marched into the kitchen. Her mouth was set and her fists were clenched. Her mother looked up. She recognised trouble.

"Yes, I know I promised you a pony when you were eleven," she said.

"Well, I'm eleven now and you —"

"Emma, calm down. Let's discuss this quietly. Your father and I have been thinking. Do you really need a pony? You've got Miss Bradshaw's to go to whenever you want …"

"Oh, Mum, if you only knew how fed up I get with that riding school and Miss Bradshaw and that bossy Doreen. All we do is go round in circles, being told to keep our toes in and our backs straight. What I need is my own pony, so that I can train him myself."

"Would you ever go to the riding school, then, if you had your own pony? The last time I spoke to Doreen she said that you could be a good rider if only you'd learn to concentrate and take in what she's trying to teach you."

"The trouble is I get bored on those riding school ponies. I'd probably go more if I had my own pony. You see, I'd have a relationship with him," Emma said earnestly.

"Relationship, indeed! And what about all the other animals we've got already. Too many, according to your father."

"They're your animals, not mine. I'm fond of them, of course, but it's your dog, and your cat and your parrot and they're your hens. You look after them. I've only got one duck, and she's as lonely as I am."

"I don't see why you're lonely ..."

"Well, I am. I love this house, but at weekends I've nothing to do. I'm miles from my friends at school, with just you and Dad and Peter, and he's no use because he's got his own friends. And in the holidays it's even worse. And now you're starting at that Citizens' Advice Bureau, too, so you won't be here a lot of the time."

"That's true."

"And you won't even let me go into town to meet my friends there now."

"Well, you know the reason why."

"Oh, Mum, please try to understand. It was just something to do, with the others. I'm very sorry about it. I meant to keep it secret, and you'd never have known if you hadn't gone into my room. I have got 'Private' on the door. Anyway, I've promised not to go with them again. I wish you'd believe me."

Emma came over to her mother and put her arms round her and her face against hers.

"You can't get round me so easily. You must know that shoplifting is wrong. What would your father say if he knew what you'd been doing?"

"But, Mum, I didn't take anything myself. Esmé gave me that lipstick and nail varnish and the other things you found. But the trouble is, I've got to do *something*. I've absolutely nothing to do when I'm not at school. They have all the shops and everything, and they won't come out here because they say it's boring, and Dad glares at them ..."

"Would you rather we fixed you up at a boarding school, then, like the other children round here?"

"No, really, I don't want to go to boarding school. I love being at home with all of you too much. I'm sure I'd run away. I like my school. It's just that I haven't enough to do. I'd be kept really busy if I had a pony to look after. And there's a place to keep him. The paddock's empty now since Mr Giles stopped renting it for his sheep. Have you thought about that? Oh, Mum, please! It would make me so happy."

Her mother sighed.

"*If* I talk to your father again, and *if* he agrees, would you promise not to let the pony stray into his garden? You know how angry he gets when he finds the hens in the vegetable garden."

"I promise, really I do. Oh, Mum, do talk to him. You can get him to do anything if you really want to. You know you can."

"Well, I'll try. Just help me peel these apples, will you, or we'll never have dinner ready by the time he comes back. And I can hear Peter now. He'll want his tea."

Six years older than Emma, Peter was at Sixth Form College. He was a tall, thin-faced, argumentative boy, who went his own way and took very little notice of his family. Emma, on the other hand, was stockily built, with auburn hair, which she wore pulled back into two bunches held together by elastic bands, an obstinate mouth and big blue eyes. She was very involved with her mother and took her side about the animals when her father, as frequently happened, complained about them.

Peter flung his case one way and his coat the other and sank into a battered armchair. "Hullo Mum, hullo Ginger, hullo Nelson – What's there to eat?"

"Make yourself a sandwich and there's tea on the stove. Supper won't be long."

"Stop calling me Ginger, you!"

"Time for tea, cocky," shrieked Nelson, an African grey parrot with one eye, who peered down at them from his aviary built into an alcove in the kitchen. It had been decorated with pictures of palm leaves and tropical foliage by one of Peter's friends.

"I'll call you cocky, then," said Peter.

"Mum, will you tell him …"

"Oh, stop teasing her. Emma, if you don't help me a bit I'll be much too tired to talk to your father about you know what."

Her father was late back from the surgery that evening.

"I could do with a stiff whisky, Alison," he called as he came in through the door.

"Pour yourself one and a gin and tonic for me. I'll bring some ice." She went into the sitting room and shut the door.

Standing outside in the hall, Emma heard her father's despairing voice. "Not another ruddy animal!" and "Surely you've got enough already!" and "Who's going to look after it – she'll be tired of it in a week." She couldn't hear everything, but finally, when she heard him shriek "A pig, I will not have a pig!", she knew that her mother had played her trump card. Anything but the oft-threatened pig; he would settle for the lesser evil. She pulled back as the door opened and caught a glimpse of him lying back in his armchair, his glass of whisky held limply in his hand, his eyes shut. Then her mother closed the door and called her into the kitchen. "You can have one, providing you promise …"

"I know, I know, he must never get into the garden. I promise."

"I'll ask Miss Bradshaw …"

"Mum, please, I don't want a riding school pony. I don't. I don't. They're trained already. I want to train my own

10

pony. They're all quite old anyway. She's bound to let you have the worst. I want a young pony, to grow up with me. Please, Mum!"

"Well, I'll ask around, and look in the local papers."

"I think I'd like a palomino, or an Arab – a thoroughbred Arab, fast as the wind. Can't you just imagine me with my hair floating behind as we gallop along. I'll grow my hair long, and I won't wear a hat ..."

"You will wear a hat! And what about the cost? And I've heard that thoroughbreds can be tricky. Anyway, I'll do my best. You'd better do some work on that old shed in the paddock and on the fence at weekends now. That should keep you busy."

Next day at school she told Esmé.

'Don't see why you're so excited," said Esmé. "I bet you'll find it's a lot of trouble. What about coming to the Arndale with us next Saturday and having a look round?"

"I'd better not. You know my dad. Not that I wouldn't like to. It's dead boring here, isn't it? Nothing interesting ever happens at school, or round us, or anywhere. I think I'll keep out of trouble, though, just for the moment. And I've got to get things ready. Why don't you come out and help?"

"Dead boring, I find the country."

There was a lot of work to do. She went down to the vegetable garden to consult Joe.

He was on his knees, planting out potatoes, with his back to her, and did not hear her come. She sat on an upturned box and watched him, remembering how, when she was little, he had had a milk round and been their milkman. He had told her he gave that up when he found lifting all those bottles too much, and now he did odd jobs for people. At first he had come only occasionally to their house, to help build a chicken house for her mother, or do weeding for her father, but now he was here almost every day, helping in the garden. She watched him kneeling there, dressed in his usual shabby blue overalls, with his frayed cuffs, his thick boots sticking out behind him, and his cap on the back of his head. She knew he had once had a wife, but he would never say what had happened to her. He lived alone now, in a cottage with a cat and a very old dog which, in the past, had gone with him on his milk round but now stayed at home and guarded the house.

"Joe," she said. "You were brought up on a farm, weren't you?"

He started slightly at the sound of her voice, looked round at her and then got slowly to his feet, holding his back. "That I was, and hard work it was, too." His red face, with its stubbly growth of grey beard, creased into a smile which crinkled his eyes and seemed to go right up to his ears. Emma loved Joe's smile.

"You'll know all about horses then. I'm going to have a pony and I've got to get the paddock ready. Come and see."

She took his hand and together they went back up the garden and through the yard.

"Mr Giles has left the place in a right old mess," she grumbled as they inspected the shed he had once used for lambing. "And the fence doesn't look too good now he's taken away his sheep wire."

"That Giles only thinks about hissen. I'll find some stakes for the wire. You see to the shed. And in the summer I'll scythe the orchard for hay for you."

Emma's face lit up. "I've always wanted to make hay, but Dad *will* cut the grass with a rotary cutter."

"Don't believe in them new-fangled machines. A good scythe is what we need – I'll tell him – save money too."

She had found an ally in Joe, and against her father too. Things were going well.

Chapter Two

A week passed, and then another week. Nobody said anything. It was getting near half-term now, which meant a whole week off school. They'd better hurry up, or else …

Then it came, the news she'd been waiting for.

Her mother was sitting at the kitchen table studying the newspaper as she came in from school, and she was underlining an advertisement.

"This one looks possible," she said, without looking up. "Fourteen hands high – that's about right, isn't it? – good character, five years old, reasonable. Shall we go and look at it?"

"What colour?" She hoped it was a palomino.

Her mother looked through the advertisement again. "Skewbald," she said finally. "What does that mean?"

"Black and white, I think, or it may be brown and white, I'm not sure. Anyway, let's go and see – I've been waiting and waiting."

"It's a Mr Riley," her mother told her father as they set off in the car the following Sunday afternoon. "A rather out-of-the-way farm in the hills."

Emma bounced about in the back as the car started to climb. Grey dry-stone walls enclosed little fields with grass cropped short by sheep. Beyond and above stretched the open moors.

"Isn't the country beautiful?" said her mother.

"What a dreadful road!" was her father's only response when they finally found the track leading between fields and up a steep hill to Mr Riley's farm. "I'll be surprised if I get away from here without a burst tyre."

Mr Riley was waiting for them when they arrived. He was small and bandylegged, with a round red face and a battered trilby clapped on his head. He opened the yard gate for them – and looked approvingly at Emma as she was introduced to him.

"Just the right size," he said. "They'll grow up together. Want to see him right away?"

They nodded.

He led them towards a field, where a brown and white pony stood on his hind legs by the fence, trying to reach a sprig of hawthorn with his large pink tongue.

"Come here, Freckles," called Mr Riley. "He's got freckled legs, see, that's why I called him Freckles."

From the depths of his pocket he produced two sugar lumps and held them out on his open palm. The pony looked round, considered the matter, and then trotted over and took them. As he did so, Mr Riley slipped the rope of the halter he was carrying round the pony's neck.

"Easily caught," he said. "No vices. I've been a jockey in my time, and I know a good one when I see one, and you're a good one, aren't you, Freckles? Stop pushing your nose into my pocket, there's no more there. Come and show what you can do."

Freckles was led into the yard and saddled and bridled.

Emma stroked his nose.

"He's got mostly white legs," she said, "with splodges on them. Are those his freckles? And half his mane is white, and half brown. And it sticks straight up. And there's white running down from his mane to his front legs, with more splodges. And he's taking notice of everything ..."

"Do hurry up, Emma," said her father. "We can see all that for ourselves."

"He's taken to you, you can see that," said Mr Riley. "Look at him nibbling your fingers, and the way he's leaning against you. He doesn't do that with everybody." He smiled at Emma. "Now, hop on his back and try him out. Go down the side of the field here and round by the path and then back up the lane to the yard. Give him a kick – make him go."

A little anxious, but excited and happy, Emma did as she was told. Freckles pricked up his ears and set off at a brisk trot, round the field and down to the river, winding below. It was a perfect early spring day, filled with gentle, watery sunlight, and Emma felt she would like to go on riding for ever. It was so different from being on a riding school pony. She rose easily to the pony's trot, and when he went into a canter she seemed to become one with him. She sensed the power in his body, and at the same time she felt totally relaxed and safe. It was like riding along in a dream.

This is the pony for me, she thought, and she was sure he responded similarly to her, so easily and happily did he carry her. He seemed to know exactly where to go, and she let him have his head. He turned for home and quickened his pace, and they came back considerably faster than they had started out, with Emma clutching his mane as they arrived in the yard. She hoped that nobody had noticed.

Her mother, however, had been watching closely. "Isn't he a bit headstrong?" she asked Mr Riley. "What about his mouth?"

"Soft as a brush – never known a better, and I've ridden plenty. Emma just needs to get used to him. Don't you, Emma?"

" 'Course I do. He's fine, absolutely fine. I can train him, Mum, I know I can."

"A first-class gymkhana pony, too. That's what you want, eh?"

"Oh, yes, that's what I want more than anything in the world." First she would win at Miss Bradshaw's, then at the Pony Club, then at the local shows, and then, who knows, she and Freckles could be chosen to compete at the Horse of the Year Show. She could just imagine herself …

"Can he jump?" she asked.

"Flies through the air like a bird. Want to try him?"

"I must be getting back," said her father. "My understanding is that all horses can jump."

"He is the first pony we've seen …" her mother began.

"Come in and have a cup of tea. Mrs Riley has it all ready for you."

"Oh, please, can we?" Without waiting, Emma set off towards the farmhouse.

"I'll just have a word with my wife first," said her father, taking her mother to one side.

"I want him, Dad, I really do." Emma called after them. Suddenly she felt desperate.

"Don't push it," advised Mr Riley. "Just …" He put his hands together and raised his eyes towards the sky. Emma shut hers and prayed. When she opened them again her parents were walking towards the gate.

"Thank you very much, Mr Riley. It's kind of you to offer us tea, but we think we should see some other ponies before we decide. My wife's not quite sure if my daughter could handle him."

"Of course I can handle him," cried Emma, running after them. "What do you think I am – two years old?" She was almost in tears.

"Into the car. I've no time to waste," said her father. Mr Riley winked at her as they set off, and she craned her neck to see Freckles one last time. He turned his head and looked at her. She was sure he wanted her to have him.

"It's no use you sulking, Emma. Freckles isn't the only pony in the world. And I did see you clinging to his neck as you came back up the lane."

They were in the kitchen, having tea.

"It was only because I'm not used to him. Mr Riley says his mouth is soft as a brush. You heard him. Mr Riley says I don't want a rocking horse. Mr Riley says ..."

"If you ask me, I think you'd be much better off with a rocking horse. I've seen some of your antics at the Pony Club." Peter was snatching a hasty meal before going out again.

"Well, we're not asking you. What none of you seems to understand is that they're hopeless ponies at Miss Bradshaw's. Hopeless! That's why I can't ride them properly. Freckles is a real pony. Freckles will make a good gymkhana pony. Mr Riley says ..."

"If I hear that name again you can take your tea out into the garden," growled her father.

"I'm only thinking of your safety," put in her mother.

Emma snorted, and Nelson gave first one wolf whistle, and then another one.

"That bird should not be on the airer whilst we're having tea, Alison," said her father, looking up, but involuntarily he whistled back. Emma thought Nelson was the only one of their pets he did like, and that was because they were both as bad-tempered as each other. "It's not hygienic. As a medical man ..."

Nelson stopped him in mid-sentence by descending on to his shoulder and nibbling his ear.

Her father tickled the top of his head and left the kitchen, his paper in one hand and cup of tea in the other, still balancing Nelson, who by this time had climbed on to his head.

"I'll never forget the scene he made when I came home with that bird, and look at him now." Her mother shook her head.

"Why has Nelson only got one eye?"

Emma had heard the story before, but she loved it.

"He was in the little local zoo with other animals when some boys raided it. I think they wanted to steal some budgies and canaries. But they reckoned without Nelson. He flew at them and shrieked so hard that the caretaker came running, but not before a boy had put out one of his eyes with a stick."

"Heroic Nelson," murmured Emma.

"Then, when they wanted to make room for an art gallery, they decided to sell the animals. They put them up for auction. I just went to have a look, that was all, but I felt sorry for Nelson. He was left to the last because he was so old and bad-tempered. Nobody wanted him."

"Funny things happen to you at sales, don't they, Mum? Do you remember when you went to buy a sofa and came back with a pianola?"

"Get on with your tea, or, if you've finished, go and do some homework," said her mother. "If you want me to try and find you a pony."

"Why bother? It's Freckles I want," Emma went out of the door, banging it behind her.

Three weeks later they were back at Mr Riley's. They had looked at other ponies, but one was too old, another had bad feet, another was too small, and another too large. And none of them had Freckles' character.

"Like to try a jump?" asked Mr Riley as he met them at the gate. "I've fixed one up. I've put on a drop noseband," he whispered to Emma as he helped her up. "You should be able to hold him better now."

"Oh, thank you. I'll be all right." She couldn't quite remember what a drop noseband was, but didn't like to tell him so. She would find out later.

"He's a beautiful jumper." Emma was glowing as she came back to them. "Please may I have him?"

"Sound in wind and limb, sharp as a needle, you won't find a better ..." Mr Riley shepherded them into tea in the white-washed farmhouse, where Mrs Riley, round and rosy like himself, was waiting with home-made scones and jam and cream as well as tea. Surely it would be all right this time, thought Emma, but she shut her eyes and prayed again, just in case.

After tea, as they sat in the sunny farmhouse kitchen, with its view of the rolling hills and the river, Mr Riley told them stories of horses he had known.

"Ever heard of a horse who smoked a pipe, Emma?" he would begin. "No! Well, you'll not credit this, but Billy – that was his name – Billy – wouldn't eat his hay after he came in from ploughing until he'd had his pipe with me. He'd have a rub down and a drink, and then he had to have his smoke. We'd sit together in the stable, all companionable like. Never known a horse like him."

"What happened to him?" Emma was hanging on to every word.

"Sad thing, swallowed his pipe, and choked to death. Couldn't save him. Then I recollect another, name of Angus ..."

"Interesting," said her father, "but I must be getting back." He did not approve of tobacco, and the kitchen was now filled with billowing smoke from Mr Riley's pipe. Mrs Riley noticed and opened the window. The story went on: "Now this Angus – Scottish he was – you wouldn't believe it, but he could whistle. That horse could whistle better than you or me. But" – another dramatic pause – "only Scottish tunes, what do you think of that? 'Bonnie Dundee' now, he knew every note ..."

21

"I must be going," Emma's father broke in. "What did you say you wanted for Freckles?"

Mr Riley got up and put a bottle of whisky on the table. "Five hundred pounds," he replied.

Her father eyed the whisky. "That's what I thought you said. Well, I'm prepared to give you three hundred."

Mr Riley was outraged. "For a beautiful pony like that – no vices, sharp as a needle, mouth soft as a brush … You can't mean it."

"I do," said her father, rising. "Come on Alison, Emma, I must get back."

Alison half rose. Emma gripped her chair. Finally Mr Riley spoke again. "I'll split the difference," he said. "I can't say fairer than that."

Her father still hesitated.

"And I'll throw in his saddle and bridle, *and* his halter."

"Done!"

Mr Riley poured out three whiskys. Her father drained his in one gulp. Her mother added water.

"I want cash, mind," said Mr Riley.

"When you deliver him."

"I'll bring him over Saturday, when I go to market."

Emma went to him and hugged him. She hugged Mrs Riley too.

"Goodbye, Freckles, see you soon," she shouted over to the paddock as they drove away.

"I only hope we've done the right thing," muttered her mother.

"I very much doubt it," replied her father, "but did you see how I got him down?"

Chapter Three

On Saturday Emma set her alarm clock for four a.m. and managed to be out of bed by six. Unaccustomed to seeing her in the kitchen at that hour, her mother's black spaniel Bodger howled and woke her father.

"What are you doing? Get back to bed at once," he shouted.

Emma went upstairs and dressed and crept out by the garden door.

Everything was ready for Freckles' arrival: straw spread on the floor of the shed, a bag of pony nuts in a corner of the garage, and an old bath in the stable which she had filled from a tap in the yard by a long hose looped over the gate. The fence was mended and she had bought a hay net to hang from a hook in the corner of the shed. Joe had given her plenty of advice.

"Seeds hay is what you want," he told her. "I'll ask round for it. Ponies are queer things: they'll eat nothing but the best if they're to thrive. The fertiliser I put on the field should have worked in by now and the grass is coming through. Just give him a hay bag at night. Time enough for nuts when the winter sets in."

She seemed to have been waiting for hours and hours, and yet no horsebox stopped at their door. Perhaps Mr Riley's forgotten, she thought. Perhaps he's sold him to someone else.

"Don't you worry," said Joe. "He'll turn up."

He was standing in the yard with Emma and her mother when an enormous cattle truck came trundling slowly along the road and pulled up by the gate with a great grinding of brakes. Mr Riley climbed down from the driver's seat and went round to the back to lower the tailboard.

"I didn't know you'd come in anything so large," said Emma. "I somehow thought you'd come with a horsebox. That's what I've been looking out for."

"Fetching some sheep back later," Mr Riley told her. "Truck'll be full then."

As the tailboard was lowered, Emma could just see Freckles, looking very small, boxed in at the far end of the truck. He whinnied and she called back to him.

"Can I lead him down?" She was dancing with excitement. "Please let me lead him down."

"Better let me do it," advised Mr Riley, spreading straw on the tailboard. "You don't want him to slip."

She watched, hardly daring to breathe, as Mr Riley led Freckles slowly down the ramp.

At last, there he was. Standing in her very own yard: her very own pony. She felt she could burst with pride. He was looking round in that interested way she had noticed before. Emma hoped he liked what he saw. She had filled her pockets with carrots, sliced sideways, as Joe had recommended, and now she slipped them on to her open palm, one by one, and fed them to him. As he munched she stroked his soft muzzle and smelt his sweet breath. Then

she walked all round him slowly, running her hand down his back to his long, thick tail and tracing with her fingers the white pattern that ran from the middle of his back, over his rump, and down his back legs. She stroked his neck and he turned and looked at her. Then she put her arms round him and breathed deeply into his nostrils.

"Really," said her father, coming in from the garden with a wad of notes in his hand. "Not very hygienic. I hope you always wash your hands after handling animals, Emma."

"Way of making friends, that is," Joe told him. "He looks a good 'un."

"Let's hope so," said her father, as he counted the notes into Mr Riley's hand.

Suddenly Freckles lifted his tail and a huge pile of manure appeared behind his back legs.

"Been in the truck a time," said Mr Riley. "I'll have that cup of coffee you promised, please, and then I must be getting on."

He and Alison disappeared into the kitchen and Emma and Joe inspected the pile of manure.

"Best get a spade from the shed and keep it here," said Joe. "You'll have plenty of that to deal with. Easiest way would be to heave it up and pile it on the other side of the wall. I can use it for the garden when it's rotted down. I'll put him in the paddock for you, and then I must be off. He looks a nice pony, but he's got a glint in his eye."

Emma went off to get a spade and a broom and cleared the manure away just in time to wave Mr Riley off.

"I'll be able to give him a good ride before lunch," she told her mother. "Joe's put him in the paddock, so I'll take the halter and go and get him. Have you any sugar lumps?"

Her mother put her hand to her mouth. "Do you know, I quite forgot. Now I've started at the Advice Bureau, I seem to have so little time for shopping. And you've used up all the carrots. Oh, you'll be able to get him with a bit of grass or something. Mr Riley said he was easy to catch. Take Bodger with you. He needs some exercise."

Half an hour later, when Emma had still not returned, her mother thought she had better go and see what had happened.

Freckles was circling round and round the paddock, with Emma and a very tired and hot Bodger in pursuit. He would allow her to approach just near enough for her to feel sure she could slip the halter round his neck, and then set off again, at a slow, steady trot, just out of reach. He seemed fresh and well pleased with himself. Emma was sweating.

"If only we had some sugar lumps," she called to her mother. "You know Mr Riley had them. Why couldn't you have remembered?"

"Well, really," said her mother, but she went off to see what she could find.

"Nuts!" she thought as she saw the bag in the garage. "They love nuts."

She put a handful in a bucket, went back to the paddock and called to Freckles. The effect was magical. He came over, put his head straight in, and they'd caught him.

With difficulty they saddled and bridled him in the yard. Mr Riley hadn't told them that it was very hard to make him open his mouth.

"What's this thing for?" asked Alison, holding up a strap.

"I think that's a what-do-you-call-it," replied Emma. "I don't expect it's important. I'll ask Doreen about it when I see her. I'll be all right without it. Help me up, will you, and hold the gate open for me."

She touched Freckles with her heels and he walked slowly through the yard gate on to the wide grass verge which ran alongside the road.

"I'll go along the verge and then cross over to the Common," Emma called back as she started to trot. "He's going beautifully."

"Is he?" her mother asked herself as she stood shading her

eyes and watching her daughter's progress. "She doesn't seem to be sitting up very straight. Whatever's wrong?"

As she watched, Emma tipped slowly sideways on to the grass, whilst Freckles, his saddle dangling between his legs, continued his steady progress without her.

Emma's father was planting out some cuttings when his wife ran to tell him what had happened.

"I knew it would be a disaster," he said as they got out the car.

"Wait! I must get some nuts or we won't catch him," Alison cried.

They found a distraught Emma running along the road. "I expect I forgot to tighten the girths," she sobbed. "Doreen said we always should, but I expect I forgot."

They caught Freckles with the help of the nuts and put his saddle the right way round again. But when Emma tried to tighten his girths he blew himself out like a balloon.

"Doreen said they do that. You have to give them a punch – Not a hard punch," she shrieked as her father, losing patience, jammed his fist into Freckles' side. It went down like a burst tyre and her father pulled the girths tight and helped her back into the saddle.

"Now perhaps I can get on with my gardening," he said as she set off again.

"Be careful," called her mother.

Freckles behaved well as they approached the Common. He walked quietly across the road and on to a wide avenue that ran between horse chestnut trees.

"Shall we try a trot?" Emma asked.

He pricked up his ears.

"I don't think we'd better canter yet," she warned him, but Freckles thought otherwise. Where the wide path narrowed, and the trees on each side began to catch at Emma's legs and clothes, and she desperately wanted just to trot again, or preferably walk, Freckles refused to slow down, however much she sat back in the saddle, and pushed out her legs, and did all the things she had been told to do. Instead he changed from a canter to a gallop.

"Oh, Freckles, stop! Do stop!" Emma cried as her hat came off, and she lost a stirrup, and overhanging branches tore at her. But he would not stop. What if she met someone walking along? She tried frantically to keep her balance.

They came to a clearing where several paths met and Freckles slowed slightly in his stride. Suddenly she remembered what Miss Bradshaw had said: "If a horse runs away with you, turn it in a circle: pull on one rein and let go of the other."

"Well, I'll have to try it." Emma shut her eyes.

She found herself lying on her back. Was she in bed, or what? But she couldn't be in bed, because she was looking at the sky. And her head hurt. She gave up trying to think.

"Is this your pony?" The voice came from a long way above her head. Emma opened her eyes with an effort and then shut them again.

"We can't have you lying there. Want me to help you up?"

She raised one hand feebly and the stranger pulled her to her feet. She wobbled and leaned against him. He brushed her down and inspected her. "No harm done, I think. No bones broken. A bit sore, eh?"

She nodded and noticed that he had hold of Freckles' rein. Freckles seemed to be avoiding her eye.

"Doctor Fairburn's daughter, aren't you? I wasn't going in that direction, but I think I should take you home. It's lucky I found you." He put her back on the saddle. She felt very sore and bruised.

Emma looked at his back. He was tall and thin and wearing a deerstalker hat, a rough jacket, and corduroys. She'd seen him before, but she couldn't remember where. They picked up her hat on the way back.

Suddenly she felt worried. If she was brought to the

door like this, after her first ride, they would know that Freckles was too strong for her. Then there would be trouble.

"Please," she said, bending down. "Please let me go into the yard on my own. Otherwise my parents might think he isn't safe."

"Well, he isn't very safe."

"I'm going to train him. He doesn't mean any harm. He's my first pony."

"Take care, then. I expect I'll find out later how you two have got on."

She dismounted, slowly and painfully, just out of sight of the house, pushed Freckles into his paddock and put away his saddle and bridle. Then she crept up to her room, where she washed her hands and face and changed her torn clothes.

"Had a good ride?" asked her mother.

"Very good," she lied.

"Only one potato left for you," Peter told her. "Thought you weren't coming."

"Greedy pig!" Emma replied automatically, but her mind was on Freckles. What was she to do about him? She decided to consult Doreen.

Chapter Four

Emma decided to set out late, after tea.

"Won't everything be over?" asked her mother. "I don't want you riding back after dark."

"I won't be long. I just want to show him to Doreen."

As she had hoped, Doreen was on her own when she arrived, putting out hay and water for the ponies that had not been turned out. She looked up briefly. Emma considered the sandy-haired, freckle-faced figure before her. She hoped Doreen would be in a good temper.

"I wanted to ask you something, Doreen. This is my new pony. He's called Freckles."

"You could have come earlier. I'd like to get home to my tea. Looks quite a good pony, though."

"He's a beautiful pony. Mr Riley said he would be fine for gymkhanas, but …"

"But what?"

"Well, I can't stop him when he wants to go."

"Oh!" Emma watched her, struggling between her

conscience and her desire to get home. She knew Doreen. She wouldn't want to have one of her pupils in an accident if she could help it.

"What's his mouth like?"

"Mr Riley said soft as a brush. He gave me this, but I'm not sure how to put it on."

"Drop noseband. You've been taught about that. Keeps the bit in his mouth. I'll try him with it anyway, and see how he goes. Watch me put it on. You can go on putting out the hay and water."

Doreen took Freckles into the big field next to the riding school and put him into a canter. When she returned she was shaking her head.

" 'Soft as a brush' indeed! He's got a hard mouth. Your Mr Riley ought to be shot. You could return him for that."

"But Doreen, I don't want to. I love him. I want him. And he's a good jumper. Can't you help me?"

"Well, we could try a stronger bit."

She rummaged about in a box.

"We'll try this pelham on him. Open your mouth, you little monkey. You've got a handful here, Emma. We'll see how he goes with this."

"Much better," she said when she returned. "If you're careful you should be all right now. By the way, Miss Bradshaw's organising a gymkhana for the end of June. Try to get him ready for that. I must be getting on now."

"Oh, thanks, Doreen. I will, Doreen. Thanks very much."

As she rode slowly home through the gathering dusk, Emma gave Freckles a lecture. "I know you don't mean any harm," she told him, "but parents don't realise that. You must try to behave or we'll both be in trouble."

He pricked up his ears and seemed to be paying attention. At any rate he was giving no trouble now, and it was wonderful to be on her own pony who picked his way carefully and didn't mind the dips or bumps or ruts in the path. Before, she had been obliged to use her bicycle and had jolted along, getting punctures from the hawthorn prickles when the hedges were trimmed. There was none of that now.

She looked contentedly around her. It was lucky that you could get to Miss Bradshaw's without going on roads, or hardly at all. Here was the lane where the gypsies camped, but they weren't there today. They'd probably been moved on. Here was big Five Acre, with a path across it, and now the Jones' farm, which had a pond, and Muscovy ducks. Tabitha was a Muscovy – the only survivor from a raid by a fox. Emma remembered bringing her home, a little duckling, from a farm holiday, and rearing her, and now she was in their orchard, feeling lonely and wanting a family, and Emma's father wouldn't hear of getting a drake. Perhaps if she could get her down to the Jones' farm one day, without anyone noticing ...

It was darker now and rather frightening as they entered the wood. There was a mysterious quality to the trees in this dusky light.

"Don't be frightened, Freckles." Emma patted his neck. "We'll just walk on quietly. No cantering today."

There were strange noises amongst the trees, and something furry scuttled along the path in front of them. Freckles shied. Emma quietened him and held the reins more firmly. He jigged from side to side for a while, but then settled down.

"It's definitely better with the pelham. I'll be able to train him properly now." Emma was dreaming again, talking to herself as they rode along. "Perhaps we'll do really well at that gymkhana. We might even come first in everything. I can just imagine Miss Bradshaw's face. 'I wouldn't have believed it,' she'll be saying to Doreen, and Doreen will reply, 'It's because Emma and Freckles have a relationship. She couldn't have a real relationship with any of the riding school ponies.' And Miss Bradshaw: 'That girl will go far; she's turning into a first class-rider.' ..."

They were coming out of the wood and the change in the light woke Emma from her dream. The last rays of the sun were piercing the roof of Mr Giles' farm like lances thrown from the sky.

"Looks really ramshackle," Emma said to herself as she rode past it. "Not surprising the shed was in such a mess after he'd had it. Wonder what he's got in those new sheds behind the farmhouse? There's a pretty awful smell coming from them."

She emerged into the main road from a track which led down to the farm and turned left along the wide verge. She was nearly home now. On the other side of the road stretched the golf course, out of bounds to horses. Her father was captain there this year.

She passed several houses set back in large gardens before reaching their own – the end one before the country really began. She loved the big, white, square house, with

its gates that shut it away from the world, and its huge yard, and Freckles' paddock to the other side of it, beyond the garage.

Freckles had quickened his pace as soon as they neared the house. He changed automatically from a walk to a trot and Emma had a lot of trouble stopping him from cantering, but she managed it. Pleased with herself, she dismounted and opened the yard gate, unsaddled him and rubbed him down, and then led him through the wicket gate at the end of the yard into the paddock.

He looked longingly at his stable, but it had been firmly barred against him by Joe.

"You're having your hay outside," she told him, hanging up his hay net. "It's spring now. You're not going in there. You make too much mess. And why did you have to do it in the yard when you got back? You could have waited. Now I'll have to heave it over the wall before I have my tea. We'll start your training tomorrow."

Freckles was already pulling at his hay and did not appear to have heard her.

Chapter Five

Emma ran into the kitchen and scraped her chair noisily as she sat down. Her father and Peter were already sitting at the table and her mother was at the stove, cooking a late breakfast of scrambled eggs. It was Saturday morning, the weather was beautiful, and Joe had promised to give Emma some help if she hurried.

"Try to be a little quieter, Emma," said her father, looking up from his paper.

"Got to be quick. Must get on with training Freckles for the gymkhana."

"Training Freckles!" Peter looked up. "I saw you the other day, careering along some lane or other, yelling 'Stop! Freckles, stop!'"

"You did not. Oh, Mum, tell him to shut up."

"Peter, leave her alone. And Emma, must you keep taking all the carrots? No sooner do I buy them than they're gone again, and you know I haven't so much time for shopping now."

"Sorry, but I need them for training." Emma gulped her tea and ran out, grabbing the last handful of carrots as she went.

With Joe's help she had rigged up some jumps and some posts in the paddock. Joe took Freckles' training very seriously and whenever he could manage it stood with a large stopwatch in his hand, timing Emma as she practised for the various races. He kept the bucket filled with water for bobbing for apples and provided potatoes from his allotment for the potato race, as Emma's father wouldn't hear of her taking any of his, and eggs for the egg and spoon race, and he caught Freckles when he had had enough of his training and bucked Emma off on to the ground.

"You've got to learn to fall soft," he said. "Or you'll do no good as a rider. Not but what you're a bad 'un," and he gave Freckles' bridle a shake as Emma picked herself up, rubbing her back and groaning.

"Well, if I ever get anywhere I'll owe it to you," she said. "I'd better take that jump again. I do wish he'd learn to keep his back legs up. He behaved so well at Mr Riley's. I don't know what's got into him."

"He's a rascal, that's what he is, and he knows these jumps won't hurt him even if he does catch his feet on them. What he needs is a good strong wall so that he'd hurt himself if he caught it. That would teach him." -

"Joe!" Her father's voice came from the vegetable garden.

"Better go. Got hoeing to do. I'll lose my job here if I spend all my time with you. Mind what I've said now, and keep him at it."

Joe shambled off and Emma was left on her own. She looked at Freckles and shook her head. Would she ever be able to turn him into the "Pony of the Year"? He loved bending. He slid in and out of the posts like an eel, and was very fast as well. But in bobbing for apples he always got at the apple before she did. In the potato race it was very difficult to hold him still while she dropped her potato into the bucket, and impossible to mount again if she had to get off. This happened in the egg and spoon race too. He was so keen that he often set off without her. And as for jumping, he could sail over jumps if he wanted to, but he had a maddening habit of dropping his back feet just a little too soon, sending the jump flying.

"Freckles, you must learn to cooperate," she told him, stroking his nose.

It was much more difficult having a pony of her own than she had imagined. All this training, and all this falling off, and all this clearing up behind him. And now he had nearly eaten down all the grass in the paddock and her father wouldn't hear of him being put in the orchard for a while. It was all very worrying. She wished she had a friend at school who liked riding and would help her, but none of them did.

Freckles jerked his head and Emma found she was still holding him. She was tired of the jumps in the paddock. Joe had suggested a wall. Where could she find one, she wondered. Then she remembered that Mr Giles had a wall, all along the back of his farm. She had ridden alongside it one day, when she and Freckles had been lost in the wood, trying to find a way out. It had been built by the Danes or the Romans or someone a long time ago – she remembered hearing about it at school – and it had a ditch running along the side of it, so it would be perfect practice for the wall and ditch jump at the gymkhana.

But how could she get to it? Mostly it had fallen down, like everything else on Mr Giles' farm, and been mended with barbed wire and wood and briars, but at the far end, towards the lane, it was a proper wall. It was no good asking Mr Giles if she could have a try, but with any luck she could get in at the farmyard gate undetected, put Freckles to a canter, and clear it before he realised what was happening. He would probably be away at the market anyway, as it was Saturday. Emma decided to risk it.

She rode Freckles quietly out of the paddock, and along the verge, and turned down the lane towards Mr Giles' farm. Better not say where she was going – she would only be told not to.

Freckles tried to pull at the hedges and dandelions as they went, but she held him back. Nobody seemed to be about. The farmyard gate was open, and Emma could not see Mr Giles' battered landrover anywhere. He must be at the market, as she had hoped. There was a clear run up to the wall from the yard, and beyond it was the wood.

"Now, Freckles," she said, "you've got to show what you can do." She dug in her heels, leaned forward, and they set off. Freckles cleared the wall and the ditch and landed on soft ground, where a ride stretched away through the woods. Emma was ecstatic.

"I knew you could, I knew you could," she cried. "We'll try again, the other way, and then go home for lunch." She took him a hundred yards down the ride and then turned him at the wall once more. "Now, Freckles, up and over."

Again Freckles sailed over the ditch and the wall. The landing was harder in the farmyard, and Emma nearly came off, but she hung on to the pony's mane and kept her seat.

"What do you think you're doing, on other people's property?"

She brushed the hair from her eyes and looking up, saw Mr Giles' large, weather-beaten face, with its bristly moustache, glaring down at her. He had parked his landrover across the gate. There was no escape that way. She turned Freckles to the wall again.

"Oh, no, you don't!" cried Mr Giles. "After them, Gyp."

Freckles almost cleared the wall, but dropped his feet a fraction too soon. Gyp jumped over the gap he had made and seized hold of Emma's shoe. Freckles stumbled into the ditch, pulling Emma with him. The dog dragged at her foot. She could hear Mr Giles encouraging him from behind. At last the shoe came off, and she and Freckles disappeared into the woods.

"I'll tell your father. I'll have you up for trespass." The shouts grew fainter and at last there was silence. Freckles slowed down of his own accord, and Emma was able to look round. The trees had closed in on them. She had no idea where she was.

They plunged deeper into the wood, but Emma found that in her fright and hurry she must have taken the wrong path. Impenetrable thickets of brambles reared up in front of them. They wove right and left to avoid them, with Emma bent low over Freckles' back. Fallen logs and twisting creepers and then a morass of slimy marsh barred their way. The wood was menacing, horrible. Freckles was spattered with mud right up to his chest. She was covered in it too, and the foot that Gyp had attacked was beginning

to swell and would hardly fit into the stirrup. Her bare arms and hands were scratched and sore.

Very little light filtered through the thick branches overhead and Emma lost all sense of direction.

"What are we to do? We must find a way out." She was crying as yet another path ended in a tangle of branches and blackberry bushes.

Freckles turned of his own accord and found another path. He seemed subdued, and hungry, grabbing any tufts of grass he could. They were in a dark, leafy tunnel, and at the far end of it, Emma could see a glint of light. They pushed on towards it, slowly, painfully. The point of light became larger and larger, and the path became a proper one, and finally they reached a clearing, where the trees had been felled in a wide circle, and the sunlight came through, strong and bright and hot. The grass was soft and short here.

Emma tumbled off Freckles and, leaving him to graze, sank back against a log. She pulled some sugar lumps from her pocket and began to suck on them. Then she closed her eyes. She was dreaming – dreaming that she was at school amongst her friends, sitting under the trees in the playground, and Esmé was tickling her, tickling, tickling.

"Esmé, please stop," she cried and opened her eyes. Then she screamed, for all over her ants were crawling, and flies were settling, and she hated ants and flies. She jumped up and picked some fern to brush them away as best she could. She was sobbing again.

"Freckles, come here," she called, but he was happy now and would not come. She and the ants between them had eaten the sugar lumps she kept for just such an emergency. There was no way she could catch him. He circled the glade two or three times, keeping just ahead of her, and then set off along a path, stopping to snatch at mouthfuls of leaves as he went.

"Oh, Freckles!" she implored. "This isn't the time to

play about. Stop, please! Where are you taking me? Please stop."

But Freckles ignored her.

Wearily she hobbled on, always a few paces behind the pony. Her foot was really hurting now. The wood had thinned out, and the path had turned into a grassy ride. Then there was a ditch, and beyond that a fence. Freckles stopped, and with a desperate spurt, she caught hold of his bridle. The land on the other side of the fence looked familiar.

"It's Mr Giles' farm," she cried. "We're back there, back at Mr Giles' farm." She would have to walk along the side of the ditch until she came to the lane leading to home. She managed to clamber on to Freckles' back with the help of a log and together they set off. The walk seemed endless, and her foot was very painful, but at last they arrived back, tired and dirty, but in time for lunch.

She unsaddled Freckles in the yard and rubbed him down with handfuls of straw, under his legs, and behind his ears, and where his saddle had been.

"That will have to do," she said. "I'll clean you up and take you round to the paddock later. I must go and have a wash."

Her mother called from the dining room for her to hurry up.

When she came downstairs there was more trouble. "How many times have I told you," asked her mother, "not to leave Freckles loose in the yard? While you've been upstairs he's been at the vegetable rack and the bird table and eaten everything he could find."

Emma put her hand to her mouth. "Not my tadpoles!" she cried. "He can't have eaten my tadpoles." But he had. The bowl was dry, and Freckles was licking his lips.

Her father showed no sympathy. "I will not go and fetch a stomach pump," he said. "And if that animal gets into my vegetable garden you can say goodbye to him. Remember that. Go and put him in the paddock."

"Why have you only got one shoe on?" asked Peter. "I bet you've fallen off again."

"Oh, shut up. No one seems to think I might be hungry."

At that moment she saw Mr Giles approaching up the garden path. "I think I'll take my lunch outside." Grabbing her plate, she retreated with Bodger to the farthest corner of the orchard.

Chapter Six

Her father had examined her foot at his surgery. Luckily she had a sprain, not a break. He had bandaged it tightly and lectured her as he did so. She was not to ride for at least a week.

At school no one was sympathetic.

"We had a really good time on Saturday," Kathy told her. "There was a fair by the racecourse, and for once we managed to win some prizes because Keith and Neil came with us. They're fantastic at shooting and knocking down coconuts."

"We've eaten so much coconut we're sick of it," broke in Joanna. "But we've saved you some."

"Oh, thanks," Emma said. "I wouldn't have been allowed to come with you, anyway. My dad gets worse and worse, and my mum is so busy advising other people she's no time for my problems. And now I can't even ride. It's going to be so boring this weekend."

The interview with her father had not gone well. Her

pocket money had been confiscated, and she had been ordered to go round and apologise to Mr Giles. She had not been yet, pleading as an excuse that her foot was too painful.

On Saturday she sat in the orchard with Bodger by her side. Solomon, a beautiful Siamese cat, light chocolate coloured with dark chocolate-coloured ears, was hunting for mice amongst the clumps of daffodils and narcissi which covered the far end of the orchard. Tabitha, Emma's pet Muscovy duck, waddled up to her. She was black and white, with red on top of her beak, and sleek and shiny, except for one wing, which stuck out untidily on one side and would not lie down. Her father said it was a swing-wing, and that they should not breed with her, but Emma was sure Tabitha was lonely and needed a family. She would lay a batch of eggs, carefully, one by one, and try to hide them, but they were always discovered by Joe, who bore them triumphantly into the kitchen, where they were made into cakes and omelettes.

"They're no use – they're not fertile – and at least one of the livestock with which this place is infested is paying for its keep," her father told her as she watched poor Tabitha wandering around outside the kitchen window, mourning for her lost eggs.

Tabitha needed a husband, if only for a day.

"I wonder," Emma mused. "I wonder if I dare."

Riding was out, and she had nothing to do. Perhaps this was the time to put her plan into operation – the plan she had made when she rode past the Jones' farm on her way back from showing Freckles to Doreen. The Joneses had ducks, including Muscovies. If she could get Tabitha down there, and leave her for a bit, she could surely find herself a husband. Then when she came back her eggs would be fertile, and if Joe would leave them alone and cooperate, and Tabitha had the sense to hide them properly and sit on them, she would have ducklings.

'Tabitha," she said. "We're going for a walk."

Emma tied a piece of string round Tabitha's neck, collected some bread as bait, and hobbled off with the duck in tow. At the garden gate Tabitha refused to go further.

"Stupid duck. I knew you'd be stupid. You'll have to go in this then." Before she knew what was happening Tabitha was pushed head downwards into a sack and hoisted over Emma's shoulder. At the gate leading to the Jones' farmyard, Emma emptied her out and went behind a hedge to watch.

Tabitha sat there bewildered. Then an elderly Muscovy waddled up to her. They began to talk – Emma was sure they were talking. Tabitha was recounting all her troubles out of the corner of her beak, and the elderly Muscovy inclined her head to listen. Then they both rose and went towards the pond, where an enormous black and white drake with bright red wattles was standing, surrounded by his wives. The elderly Muscovy went up to him. Tabitha stood demurely to one side. Then ... Emma was sure it would be all right now. She'd leave them together and hope that Tabitha came home on her own. It wouldn't be her fault if she didn't have babies now. She'd done her best.

It was Peter who brought Tabitha back, that evening.

"She was trying to get out of the Jones' farmyard," he told his mother. "Don't know how she got there. I opened the gate and caught her. She's looking rather bedraggled, with most of her topknot chewed off. They've no right to try to steal our duck."

Emma said nothing.

"Why can't I have a ride?" Emma asked her father next day. "Freckles needs exercise."

"I'll put you in plaster if you do," he warned her. "It's quite a bad sprain and a jolt could do a lot of harm. But you could try a little gentle walking."

"Well, I don't know what I'm going to do."

"There are hundreds of things you could do," her mother told her. "You could go and apologise to Mr Giles for one thing. He won't give you your shoe back until you do. Take this stick and walk round there. Bodger can go with you: he needs a walk."

Emma sighed and went off reluctantly. It was so much pleasanter riding than walking.

When she finally got to Mr Giles' farm he was nowhere to be seen.

"Probably down with his sheep somewhere," she told Bodger. "Just as well, really. Gyp might have attacked you, like he did me. Let's go round the back and see what he's got in those sheds with funnels coming out of the top."

The sheds were quite new. Mr Giles had previously had chickens scratching about in his farmyard, and a tumbledown barn where they laid their eggs. Now they were nowhere to be seen, but from the sheds came a low continuous sound of cooing, a kind of cackling, only it wasn't exactly cooing or cackling. The smell Emma had noticed before was much worse here. She approached cautiously. One of the doors was slightly ajar. She pushed it open further and went in.

The shed was lit by low-power electric bulbs. In the dim light which they gave out she saw rows and rows of hens sitting in little cages, placed tier upon tier. They were peering out, scarcely able to move, unable to stretch their wings, or perch, or scratch. Their necks were rubbed raw from craning through the bars. There was bare wire on the floor of their cages. Their droppings went through on to a belt, which was dirty and smelly. In front of each row was a continuous feeding trough containing mash and water. Some hens had collapsed and appeared to be dead, or dying. Some had lost almost all their feathers. And from all of them came a continuous low-pitched cry as they pushed their necks this way and that. Dust and feathers lay on the floor and made the air difficult to breathe.

Emma walked in tears down the rows. Her mother's hens were so happy, glossy and healthy, as they scratched about. She had never imagined anyone could keep birds like this. She had never seen anything so dreadful.

She walked back very thoughtfully. Something must be done, but who could she ask to help?

"You're very quiet," her mother said to her at lunch. "What are you thinking about?"

"I saw a most dreadful sight." She was nearly crying again as the memory of what she'd seen came flooding back. Everything was blurred and she rubbed her fists into her eyes.

"Well, what did you see, for goodness sake?" Peter asked, his mouth full of potato.

"I went round to apologise to Mr Giles, but he wasn't there. So I went round the back, to look at some sheds I'd noticed one day when I was riding, because they smelt. And I went in and found hens all in little cages, their necks rubbed raw, that's what I saw. They were making such a sad noise – and the smell, and the dust, it was dreadful."

"Battery hens! Sounds a right sort of farmer!" Peter was indignant. "We can't have that sort of thing round here. You get a plan of the place, Emma, and we'll get the Animal Rights Brigade on to him. There's a branch at our school."

"Would you really help, Peter?" Emma was happy again.

"I won't have you jeopardising your exams, Peter, by any nonsense of that sort," her father put in. "Just leave Mr Giles to look after his own affairs. I don't want you involved in anything illegal."

Emma's mother looked out of the window. Through a gap in the trees she could just see her bantams scratching about at the bottom of the garden.

"I don't like the man," she said. "Do you remember when he refused to let me look after that motherless lamb and it died? Mr Giles leases his farm from Lord Osberton, and I know he would object to keeping hens in that way on any of his land. Perhaps we'd better let him know. Animals shouldn't be confined like that. My bantams are happy all day long, and they don't do any harm."

"Oh, don't they? What about when they get out? And how much do your eggs cost, when by some lucky chance you happen to find any of them? About a pound each, I should think."

"They're in this pudding anyway, Jim," she said. "And profit isn't everything."

Just then the telephone rang.

"If that's for me ..." he said, going to answer it. It was.

He put his head back round the door. "I might be some time."

"Your father doesn't get much time for what he wants to do when he's on call. It makes him irritable. He doesn't mean all he says," their mother told them.

"Well, I know what I want to do." Emma jumped up. "Get Freckles and give him some grazing in the orchard while Dad's out. He's eaten almost all the grass in his paddock."

"Make sure he's on a halter and doesn't wander on to the lawn," her mother warned her. "Peter, you'd better get on with some work. And as for me, do you know what I'm going to do?"

"No!" they chorused.

"Clear the table and stack the washing-up machine. Either of you want to help me?"

When she looked round, the room was empty.

Chapter Seven

"**M**um, I've brought Alan along," Peter called as the two boys came into the yard, propped their bicycles against the wall and went down into the orchard. It was a week later, a beautiful early June day.

Alison greeted them warmly, wiping flour from her hands.

Emma was lying on a rug reading. Her foot was still bandaged but more lightly than before.

From his outside aviary Nelson shrieked, "Shut the gate," and "Belt up, cocky."

"You did a good job on his inside aviary," Alison told Alan. "He really seems to think he's in the jungle when he's in it. I hear you're going to art college in September."

"If I get my A levels, and you know I'm not much good at anything except painting and drawing."

"Well, that'll be one A level you'll get, at any rate."

Peter and Alan sat down on the grass beside Emma.

"I'm fed up with this wretched ankle," she told them. "I can't get on with Freckles' training, and the gymkhana's only a month away."

"What are you going in for?" Alan asked. He was a tall boy, taller than Peter, with a thin face and dark hair, which he brushed up into a peak, and long, thin hands. He was Emma's favourite amongst Peter's friends.

"Oh, bending – he's good at that – and the potato race, and the egg and spoon, and musical hats, and jumping, and I'd like to go in for the fancy dress, but I haven't got one, and anyway I can't think what to be."

She lay back and closed her eyes. Then she heard Alan's voice from above her head. "I could design you one. It would be practice for me."

"Oh, would you?" Emma sat bolt upright, her eyes shining with excitement. Then her face fell. "But who would make it?" she asked. "I'm no good at sewing, and I'm sure Mum's too busy."

"I'll make it too: I could submit it for the practical. I'm going in for design."

Emma put her arms round his neck.

"Easy! Easy! You'll embarrass the chap. Can you sew then?" Peter asked.

"Of course. I've made dresses for my mum, but she always has some excuse not to wear them."

Alison laughed. "Make me one, and I'll wear it to the CAB. That should shake them up."

The telephone rang.

"Got to go," Emma's father said, coming out on to the lawn. "They must think that we doctors are robots. I may be away some time." He nodded coldly to Alan and went out of the gate.

"Dad doesn't think you're a good influence on me," Peter told him. "I think it's your hair."

"What's wrong with his hair? I like it." Emma was indignant.

Then she looked at her mother. "Can I get him?" she asked.

"Well, if you keep him tethered ..." Alison began, but Emma had gone.

She brought Freckles to join them, and gradually all the other animals gathered round – Solomon, and Bodger, and Tabitha – and Nelson called to them from his perch.

"What shall I be? What shall I be? Something quite different – not a shepherdess, or Red Riding Hood. Something strange and horrible. Let's all sit and think."

"What about a nightmare?" asked Alan. "You know, a pun on mare. Rather good, I think."

Peter burst into raucous laughter.

"What's so funny?"

"Have you ever looked at Freckles?"

"No, but ...."

"Well, have a look."

"I can't see anything odd."

"He's a gelding, not a mare, you idiot. You artists, I thought you were supposed to be observant." Peter put his arm affectionately round his friend's shoulders.

"Oh, well, you could always cover that part up. Anyway, if you don't like it, *you* think of something."

"I've got it," Alison cried, after a long silence. "We went to a party the other day and they had canapés and bits of bacon wrapped round prunes, and do you know what they're called? 'Devils on Horseback'."

"Perfect!" Alan was ecstatic. "I'll do you a 'Devil on Horseback' fancy dress. You'll have a wonderful devil's mask, and a tail, and ..."

"What is that pony doing here? I come back to fetch something and what do I find? Take him round to the paddock at once," Emma's father blazed.

Joe appeared from the vegetable garden and offered to lead Freckles back.

"I told you to get on with the hoeing, not mess about

53

with animals. One of these boys could do it, I should think."

"There's one good thing about medicine," Emma said when her father had gone off again and her mother was in the house making tea. "It does keep doctors occupied most of the time. I don't know how Joe puts up with him."

"His bark's often worse than his bite, you know."

Next day at school Emma told her friends about the fancy dress. It was hard work making them promise to come and watch the gymkhana.

"Well, I might," Esmé said, "if we don't go to the sea for the day. It's the Whit holiday, you know."

"I don't want to see a lot of silly snobs playing silly games," Joanna chimed in.

"Peter says he'll bring his friends. Some of them are quite good-looking."

"Big deal! But I expect I'll be there."

Only Kathy really seemed to want to come.

Alan came round with the fancy dress on the evening before the gymkhana.

"It's certainly different," Emma said after she had inspected it.

"Well, you wanted something different."

It was a tight fit: a black suit, slashed with red, the feet and arms ending in blood-red claws. It had a long tail with bristles on the end, and the mask had fangs, pointed ears and slant eyes. Emma tried it on and found she had great difficulty seeing anything through the mask. She struggled out of it again, red-faced and perspiring.

"I hope I don't catch Freckles with the claws and make him bolt. And that the tail doesn't get twisted round his legs. And that I can see enough not to go the wrong way by mistake ..."

"Oh, for goodness sake. Do you want the fancy dress or don't you?" Peter was angry and Alan looked hurt.

"Of course I do. It's wonderful. Thank you very much."
But Emmma remained doubtful.

Later that evening, sitting on the kitchen floor in front of a large bowl of soapy water, with Freckles' tack spread out all around her, she confided in her mother.

"Never mind," Alison said. "You'll have to wear it now, and things may turn out better than you think. You'd better make sure Freckles is securely fastened in and get to bed. You'll have to be up early tomorrow. We'll be coming to watch in the afternoon."

Her mother left the kitchen, and Emma sat on, dreaming. Perhaps the judges would love her fancy dress. They might say, "How original! No one else has ever thought of anything like that." And everyone would cheer. And it wouldn't split. And Freckles would behave. He had been brushed and combed and his hooves oiled: she couldn't do any more.

She went off to bed and quite forgot to shut him in.

Emma seemed to be in a boat, being tossed this way and that. She opened her eyes and looked up into her father's angry, unshaven face. He was shaking her to try to wake her up.

"Whatever's the matter?" she asked sleepily.

"Matter! If you go and look at my vegetable garden you'll see what's the matter."

"It's fine. I got Mum a lettuce from it last night. Do let me go to sleep again."

"You're getting up this minute. Not only did you leave the gate open but you left Freckles in the yard. Just go and look at the damage he's done."

Her father was dancing up and down with rage.

It was barely light. Emma flew down the stairs and out of the kitchen door. Bodger and Solomon greeted her as she passed and Bodger followed her out, glad to have been released from his basket so early, but Nelson kept his head firmly under his wing.

She met Freckles as he was coming back through the gate to the vegetable garden, trailing between his legs the trellis meant for the peas, a lettuce protruding from his mouth. Looking through the gate, Emma saw a scene of utter devastation: deep hoofprints everywhere, plants uprooted, neat rows of beanpoles smashed, radishes and spinach leaves half bitten and tossed aside. She caught at Freckles' halter and tried to disentangle the string from round his legs.

"I forgot! I forgot! I did mean to shut him in last night. I just forgot!" she called desperately up to her father, who was watching her from his bedroom window.

"Forgot! That's all you ever do, forget! Well, it's not good enough. Do you want to kill me? That animal has undone months of work, in just one night. What are we to do with you?"

Her mother's head appeared beside his.

"You'd better go, Emma, as quickly as possible," she said. "I'll come down to see you off. Your father will talk to you later. Do come back to bed, Jim. You've got a heavy morning."

"Heavy morning! Little does she care about that. When I'm in my grave she might be sorry ... When you're all paupers ..."

"Oh, don't be so melodramatic! Go and get ready, Emma. I'll be down soon."

"You'll pay for this. You'll replant that vegetable garden single-handed ..." She could still hear her father's voice as she led Freckles back up the steps into the yard, shut the garden gate and set about grooming him all over again.

"Oh, Freckles!" she groaned. "Just look at the state you're in, and I bet you've been rolling too, haven't you? You don't mind how much trouble you get me into, do you? And you don't care that I haven't even had breakfast yet."

He nuzzled her palm with his nose and she leaned

against his dirty shoulder, brush in hand. It had been her fault: she shouldn't blame him. She tied him to the gate and, when he was clean again, with his feet oiled and his mane and tail washed, she went in to get some breakfast.

Chapter Eight

"I do hope everything goes well, Emma. Are you sure you've pulled the girths tight?" her mother said as she waved her goodbye.

"You'll never let me forget that, will you? See you later," Emma called back over her shoulder. "And please tell Dad I'm very sorry and I don't want to see him in his grave."

She set Freckles to a trot. She could control him better now, there was no doubt about that. Of course if he decided to go one way and she the other he usually won, but he hadn't run away with her for quite a time. This afternoon would show what they could do together, and then her parents would be proud of her. Here she was, riding to the gymkhana on her own pony, instead of having to take one of Miss Bradshaw's. It was quite different, and very exciting. She patted Freckles' neck.

"You can canter now," she told him, and then wished she hadn't, because he refused to slow down when she wanted him to. They arrived at the entrance to the gymkhana field at a gallop, with Emma clinging to his neck.

"What is that child doing?" Miss Bradshaw cried as Freckles suddenly stopped short by a group of ponies and Emma shot over his head. Doreen caught his rein.

"You don't seem to have quite got over your problem," she said. "Are you sure you're going to be all right today?"

"Oh, yes, Doreen." Emma picked herself up. "I've been training him. He's a bit excited now, but he'll be fine, really he will." She rubbed her shoulder.

Anne, a supercilious girl whom Emma hated, looked down on her from her pony Starlight. "He looks to me a bit like a gypsy pony," she said.

"He's not a gypsy pony. He's Irish," Emma replied as she took charge of Freckles again.

David was there, on his pony Trigger. She liked David. He always had trouble controlling Trigger.

"How do you like having your own pony?" he asked.

"Wonderful. He's a bit of a handful, but I'm training him."

"You're lucky not to be at boarding school. You'll be able to have a lot more time with him. Hope you do well."

"You too."

She remounted and went off to have a look round. The gymkhana was being held in a farmer's field, which had been cropped short by sheep. Oak, ash and may trees sheltered it from the road. The may blossom was almost over, but its musty scent still hung in the air. The main gymkhana ring was enclosed by rope, slung between posts, and all round it bales of straw had been placed as seats. There was a smaller collecting ring, and a piece of ground at the back for practising jumping. The day was bright, but cold.

There weren't many spectators yet, and Emma inspected the tea tent, the prize tent, with all the rosettes laid out, and the two ice cream vans. She bought an ice cream, and Freckles helped himself to some cones stacked in a box behind the van. She got away before the man noticed. In the distance she saw Miss Bradshaw in a grey costume and heavy brogues.

She went to get her number.

"Number 7," Doreen told her as she tied it round her waist. "That should be lucky. What are you entering for?"

"Everything."

Doreen raised her eyebrows. "Better go into the collecting ring, then."

Emma scrutinised her rivals. There was Anne, on the brushed and shining Starlight. She was dressed in riding breeches, and boots, with a cravat and what looked like a brand-new riding hat. She was even wearing a hair net. Emma was in well-worn jodhpurs and Peter's old jacket, as her mother had refused to buy her a new outfit. Then there was David on Trigger: she felt she could cope with him. And then there was a rather fat boy called Mark on a rather fat pony. They wouldn't be very fast, but they'd probably be steady. There were some others she knew slightly, all of them girls. Nobody from her school: her school didn't go in for riding.

Apple bobbing was first.

"I don't suppose we'll even get beyond the first heat in this one," Emma confided in David. "Freckles always gets his head into the bucket and eats the apple."

This occasion was no exception. After a great fight with Freckles, from which both emerged dripping wet, Emma had hold of a very small piece of apple, which she bore to the finishing post. It was not enough. Mark won that heat.

In the sack race Freckles refused to trot along quietly beside her when she got into her sack. He insisted on going round in circles and upsetting the other competitors. She was disqualified.

The fancy dress was next, before the lunch interval.

Afterwards there was bending and musical hats and egg and spoon, and then the jumping. Emma was tired and despondent by this time. She went over to talk to her friends, who had just arrived.

"How have you done so far?" asked Esmé.

"All right, quite all right."

"Liar! We've been watching you." Peter said. He and Alan had come up to help with the fancy dress. "You haven't done at all well."

"He's getting settled in. Just wait until the bending. He's marvellous at that."

"You can change in our box for the fancy dress," called Doreen.

When Emma emerged, very hot inside her mask, there was a gasp. As she approached Freckles he tried to bolt. Doreen held him back. "Whatever are you?" she asked.

"I'm a 'Devil on Horseback'. You know – a prune wrapped round with bacon. Alan made the dress. Do you think they'll like it?"

"Well, I wish you luck anyway." Doreen looked at Alan. He had an earring in one ear, his hair brushed high up on his head and gelled, and was wearing a black, fringed suit of his own devising, with a scarlet scarf and soft green leather boots. He looked very different from the mothers who were fussing round their children as they emerged from their horse boxes.

"I knew it! Just look at them!" Emma had pulled off her mask and, very red in the face, was watching the other competitors. "A fairy! Red Riding Hood! A knight! A shepherdess! They're all the same, always."

Joanna and Kathy and Esmé had wandered up, dressed in their shortest skirts, their hands over their mouths.

"And stop giggling, you lot. You know Peter, and this is Alan, who made my fancy dress."

"What a sight!" Anne, as Red Riding Hood, her cloak and hood becomingly arranged, was being helped on to

Starlight by her mother.

"Just you wait," shouted Emma as, with a loud splitting noise, she was placed on Freckles and her mask and tail were adjusted. Freckles tried to bolt again, but Peter stopped him.

"All competitors into the ring, please." The call came through the loudspeaker.

"You're going the wrong way, you know," said Kathy.

"Well, if I can't see a thing, what do you expect?" came a muffled voice from within the mask.

"You'd better lead her, Alan," said Peter. "I'll go and tell the others to whip up a cheer. I'll come and help if you need me."

Help was soon needed. The little procession, headed by the knight, wound slowly round the ring. The band struck up, and the knight's pony broke into a trot. The others followed. But Freckles did more than follow. He had decided he wanted to be leader, and Alan, pulled along behind, could do nothing to stop him. Then the devil's tail somehow became entangled with Freckles' own, and the devil's claws dug into him as Emma tried to right herself. This was more than Freckles could stand, and with a tremendous buck he deposited Emma in front of the judges' stand.

"And what are you supposed to be?" asked one of the judges.

"A devil on horseback," whispered Emma.

"Then perhaps you'd better get back on your horse," said another judge, "and not hold everything up."

Peter came and helped her up again and led Freckles after that, but although all his friends cheered Emma and Freckles every time they passed, and Esmé and Kathy and Joanna clapped them loyally, when they were finally judged, Red Riding Hood was first, and the Devil on Horseback was placed last.

"What went wrong?" Emma asked her mother, who had

just arrived. She was slithering out of her suit.

"Wrong place. Wrong people," said her mother. "Nothing wrong with the fancy dress. Hullo, you there." She put her arms round Emma's friends. "I'm glad you're here to cheer her up. Let's go over to all the people Peter brought and thank them for coming."

Peter and Alan and most of their form were sitting in a noisy circle drinking coke. They had been cheering Emma, for all the good it had done.

"Hooligans! Yobs! Dressed in scruffy jeans and sneakers. Miss Bradshaw shouldn't let them in." Anne and her mother passed by, arm in arm, speaking loudly enough for them to hear.

"Snobs!" shouted one of the boys.

Colonel Withington, who had been chief judge at the fancy dress, came up to Emma's mother. "These lads troubling you?" he asked.

"Not at all. They happen to be my son's school friends."

"That'll teach him," said Emma. "Now for bending. Freckles is marvellous at bending. Just you wait and see." She had left Freckles tied to the horsebox and went off to collect him.

"You can't keep her down," Kathy said admiringly. "It's the same at school. She bobs up again like a cork."

Freckles did win his heat at bending, twisting in and out of the poles like an eel, with not an inch to spare. In the final, Emma had Anne on her right and David on her left. She and Anne were running neck and neck as they reached the finish. Then Freckles gave Starlight a small shove, just enough to unbalance her, and raced into second place, narrowly beaten by David. Doreen was judging, since Miss Bradshaw was talking to a parent. She put David down to third place, as he had missed two posts, and declared Emma the winner, with Anne second. Emma's father had arrived, and she saw him actually clapping as she trotted round the ring in first place. Freckles had won his first red rosette.

The band at the end of the field now started to play. It was time for musical hats.

"I've got a chance if only I can control him," Emma thought. "If only he'll circle a post long enough for me to get my hat on it. He's had enough training, goodness knows! That circling round he did in the sack race probably shows he's remembered." She took a firm grasp of the reins and gripped tight with her knees as they went into the ring. Anne came up alongside her on Starlight. "Your pony bumped mine in the bending – you know he did. I should have won."

"No he didn't."

"He did. You're Doreen's favourite, that's why you won."

"I'm not."

"You are."

"Bighead."

"Liar. Just you watch out."

Conscious that her parents were watching, and willing with all her might for Freckles to do well, Emma circled the posts to the music, and when it stopped made a wild dash to the nearest one with her hat in her hand. She managed to get it on, once, twice, three times, four times, five times. Somehow she managed it. They won't be able to say I can't control him now, she thought.

At last there was just one post left, and only she and Anne were circling it, watching, listening. When would the music stop? It seemed an eternity before it did. Both ponies made a dash for the single post, and again Freckles outmanoeuvred the heavier Starlight. Emma got her hat over the post first. She had won again.

Anne was furious. "He got in my way – you know he did. Just as I was about to put my hat on the post he put his head in the way. It's not fair. I'm telling my parents."

"Just because you don't know how to ride, stupid!"

Anne rode off in a terrible rage. Freckles now had two red rosettes pinned to his bridle. Emma took him over to show her parents, and her father bought her an ice cream. Then she rode off to see her friends.

"Keep it up," Esmé said. "That Anne needs taking down a peg."

"I rather fancy the boy on the brown pony," Kathy told her.

"Oh, that's David. He's nice, but he's at boarding school."

"And I like Alan," Joanna said.

"Better take up art then. I must go. Egg and spoon now. Then there's the interval for tea, and then the jumping."

Emma went off to collect her egg.

She won her heat by going very carefully. But she would have to be fast now to stand a chance, as Anne and David were both in the final again. Anne put herself as far as possible from Freckles, and glared at them both. Emma noticed that Miss Bradshaw had stationed herself on her shooting stick between the lines of ponies.

"I bet she's been told to watch out for me," Emma thought. "Stupid old thing. But I hope Freckles does go straight."

She collected another egg, placed her thumb firmly upon it, turned Freckles and, when the whistle went, dashed for the finishing line. But unfortunately, Freckles decided to take a short cut. He had been on the outside and was heading instead for the middle. He charged in front of the other ponies, straight towards Miss Bradshaw, seated alone on her shooting stick. Emma tugged and shouted, but she could do nothing to stop him. There was a scrunch, and a bump, and down Miss Bradshaw went, whilst Freckles continued on his headlong course. Looking back, Emma could see her spreadeagled on the ground, her brogues sticking up in the air.

Doreen caught Freckles' bridle as he crossed the finishing line. "You're in trouble, I'm afraid," she said.

"Oh, Freckles! You've really done it now."

Emma looked over aghast at the ring of spectators that had gathered round Miss Bradshaw. Her father was kneeling down, examining her. It *would* be her father, wouldn't it, she thought. Emma had entertained a wild hope that he and her mother might have gone home, but no, there he was, helping Miss Bradshaw up, and supporting her towards the tea tent, with her mother on the other side, looking very serious and anxious. She got off Freckles and put her head against his shoulder.

"Bad luck," Kathy whispered. "The others have gone, but I've brought you this." She slipped a very sticky doughnut into Emma's hand.

"You shouldn't be allowed here. You're a danger to the public," Anne shouted to her as she passed.

"It's the old trout's fault for being there," David said as he dismounted. "I think they're running the race again after tea." He smiled at Kathy.

"Oh, David, I don't want to stay – I couldn't stay now. Please tell my mum and dad I've gone home and that I'm sorry."

What on earth would happen now?

Chapter Nine

The bright day suddenly turned to rain and Emma was soaked by the time she arrived home. Wet, shivering and bedraggled, she rubbed Freckles down and put him in his stable with some hay and water and then went into the kitchen. Peter was at the table eating hot buttered toast and reading a comic.

She put some bread into the toaster herself and took off her wet coat and shoes. Then she let down the airer to get a sweater to wear. Peter had put Nelson there, and he came down with it crying "Up the Buffs" in a throaty, bass voice.

"He's imitating that Osborne man who comes to visit Dad," said Peter. "Here, Nelson." He lobbed a piece of toast at him. Nelson missed it, and Bodger bore it off to his basket.

"Guess what happened after you left," she said, gulping down hot cocoa and toast.

"Covered yourself with glory, I expect." Peter,

absorbed, did not look up.

"Anything but! Well, I did at first – Freckles won two red rosettes, and Dad was watching and even bought me an ice cream, but then disaster struck. You'll never guess what happened!"

"Do hurry up." Peter was anxious to go on reading. "What happened?"

"Freckles and I knocked Miss Bradshaw flat!"

"No! Were the parents still there?"

"Naturally. Dad went to her rescue, with Mum walking behind holding the little black bag. I decided it was time to go. I thought they'd be back before now. Don't know what's keeping them. At least I think I do know. They'll have been talking to Miss Bradshaw about me not being able to control Freckles. And then there's what happened in the vegetable garden – did you know about that?"

"Couldn't help hearing. Dad was shrieking all over the house – 'That pony's got to go, he's got to go – I can't stand any more – it's him or me' – that sort of thing. I'm surprised he turned up at the gymkhana."

"I told you, he was coming round. He bought me an ice cream, and then this had to happen."

Just then they heard two cars drawing up.

"Both together! I can't face them. I'm off. Bring me up some more to eat, please. I'm still starving. Four knocks. And let me know what they're saying." She picked up her mug of cocoa and headed for the stairs.

Some time later someone tried the handle of her bedroom door. Then there was a single knock.

"Emma!" It was her mother's voice.

Then she sneezed. She didn't mean to, but one enormous sneeze was followed by another, and then another.

"Emma, if you've caught cold riding home in the rain go and have a hot bath immediately. We want to talk to you later."

Emma gave another loud sneeze.

Later there were four knocks on the door. Emma opened it and Peter handed her a large plate of bread and cheese and tomatoes.

"Dad's pacing around," he told her. "And Mum's saying she always knew Freckles was too strong for you. They're planning something, I think."

"I bet they are. Thanks, Peter." She locked the door again.

Emma lay on her bed thinking. Miss Bradshaw and Doreen would have talked to them. They would have told them that she could not control Freckles. So her parents would tell her they had decided to sell him and try to get her a quieter pony. But she didn't want a quieter pony. She wanted Freckles. They might even say she couldn't have a pony at all any more, and that she would have to go back to the riding school. And she couldn't bear that! So what could she do? There was only one thing for it – run away!

"I'll run away," she shouted to her ceiling light. "I'll run away and join a circus. I'll show them! I'll make them sorry! I'll go tonight. I don't want to see them again, ever!"

Her mother knocked on her door again.

"I don't want any supper," Emma shouted. "I've gone to bed."

"We'd better leave her alone tonight," she heard her mother say. "We'll talk to her in the morning."

"Oh, will you? That's what you think! I won't be here in the morning," Emma thought to herself.

She made her preparations. Into her rucksack went the bread and cheese and tomatoes, her pyjamas, another sweater, all the money she had saved – £3.10 – and some more pants and jeans. She took two blankets from her bed and rolled them up – one for her and one for Freckles. Then she sat and listened.

It was Saturday night. Her parents usually had people in for bridge, if her father wasn't on call.

She heard voices in the hall. The Pargeters had arrived.

"We've been brushing up on our system," she heard Mrs Pargeter say.

Then her mother's voice: "We've hardly been playing at all. Come in and have a drink."

The sitting room door closed.

"Now for it," Emma told herself.

She tiptoed into the kitchen, stuffed some carrots and apples into her rucksack, ate two of the sandwiches prepared for the bridge players, and looked round for some cord to tie the blankets on to Freckles. She found some outside the kitchen door, and also a large torch. That would do to light the way. She sneezed again, so she stuffed a wad of tissues in as well.

"Goodbye Nelson. Goodbye Bodger. Goodbye Solomon," she whispered. "Don't know when I'll see you again."

Tabitha waddled up to the steps leading from the yard.

"I hope you have a family, Tabitha," she told her. "Guard your eggs carefully. I've told Joe not to collect them."

Then she went round to the paddock to saddle and bridle Freckles. She might be seen if she did it in the yard. Tying the torch between his ears was the hardest job, but at last it was done. She put the blankets in front of the saddle and her rucksack on her back. It was a fine night now, but it was cold, so she put on two sweaters and her anorak.

She had sometimes seen brightly painted gypsy caravans passing slowly along the road by her parents' house, with ponies looking just like Freckles plodding along behind. They camped on the wide verges of the lanes which ran off the main road. Perhaps she would find one, and they would tell her how to join a circus. But now it was time to go. She led Freckles out on to the verge and then clambered on to his back. The lights of the house seemed friendly as she looked round, and it was very sad to have to leave. She felt forlorn and misunderstood.

She urged Freckles to a trot, but he kept trying to turn for home: he had no wish to be out again after his long day at the gymkhana. It was growing quite dark now, and Emma leaned forward and turned on the torch before taking the right turning up the lane past the Jones' farm. She hoped she would find gypsies camping on one of the wide verges further on.

"Never mind, Freckles." She talked to him as she rode. "You're so clever, you're bound to be a great success when we join a circus. I'll learn how to stand on your back without falling off, and wear a spangled top and ballet skirt, and we'll go round and round the ring, faster and faster ..."

Then, suddenly, disaster struck for the third time that day. They were well past the Jones' farm, and trotting on steadily, when a tractor appeared in the lane. Freckles hated tractors. He tried to turn and bolt for home, but the lane at this point was too narrow, with banks and thick hedges on either side. Terrified, he crashed through a weak point in the hedge, and Emma caught a fleeting glimpse of the Jones' farm boy's astonished face over the tractor wheel. Then Freckles shot off, clearing ditches, crossing fields and jumping hedges. Emma clung to his neck, imploring him to stop. She lost her stirrups, and her hat. Then they plunged into a wood and the branches bore down on them, like cruel claws trying to drag her off. She put up a hand to save herself, and felt her arm snap.

An excruciating pain shot through her and she tumbled to the ground. She felt her head hit a stone and everything went black.

Much, much later she opened her eyes. She was in her own bed at home, and one arm, in heavy plaster from the shoulder downwards, was impossible to lift. Her head ached. She felt hot and stuffy. Her chest ached too. Peter was looking down at her.

"What happened?" she asked. "What's happened to my

arm?"

"You fell off Freckles and broke it. Don't you remember anything about it?"

"Not really. What was I doing?"

"You tried to run away, I think. Mr Jones rang up and said that his boy had seen you as he was coming back late on the tractor."

"What's happened to Freckles?"

"He came home, with blankets strapped to him and a torch all upside down between his ears. He was in a terrible state, whinnying and pawing the ground. Mum and Dad went to look for you in the car."

"Did they find me?"

"No, Freckles did. I tried to quieten him, and then I thought he might want to show me where you were, so I got on his back and he took me, over hedges and ditches. I've never had such a ride: I'm still sore all over."

"Poor Peter. You must have looked funny, with your feet almost touching the ground."

"Anyway, there you were lying unconscious in a wood. I hoisted you on to Freckles' back and brought you home. Don't you remember anything?"

Emma shook her head and cried out with the pain.

Just then her father and another doctor entered the room, and Peter went out. They were looking at some X-ray plates, and her father's face was grave.

"There's definitely no skull fracture," the other doctor was saying. "You can rest assured of that. Bruising of the head, but no fracture. And the arm's set well. She needs complete rest for a while, and no worries. I'm sure you were right to bring her home."

She heard them come over to her bed. She kept her eyes shut. Her father opened one lid, and then the other.

"You little monkey, Emma," he said suddenly. "You can open your eyes, can't you?"

She looked at him.

"What would you do with a child like that?" he asked. "Ruined my only good hand at bridge last night, and now she's trying to fox us."

Then he put his hand very gently on her forehead. "Hurts, does it?" he asked.

She tried to nod and winced with the pain.

"Better not give her anything for it," said his friend. "Just complete rest. You were lucky, Emma. You had a very narrow escape. Your parents were worried to death about you. Just don't try to move and you'll be all right."

They both left the room and she shut her eyes again and drifted off to sleep.

Her mother was there, sitting by the bed when she woke up.

"Don't try to talk," she said.

"But I want to. I don't remember, but Peter told me what happened. What's happening to Freckles?"

"There are a lot of things we've got to discuss when you're better."

"What things?"

"Wait and see."

"About Freckles."

"Wait and see."

Chapter Ten

What did her mother mean? Wait and see? Emma tried to puzzle it out, but her headache made thinking impossible. She closed her eyes and was soon asleep again.

She could not get up, even to go to the bathroom. She could not have visitors. A nurse came in twice a day to see to her, turn her over, wash her, and give her a bedpan. "Me! Being treated like this!" she protested, but she could do nothing about it. Her head hurt so much when she lifted it that she gave up trying. Mostly she lay and dreamed, and at other times her mother fed her and read to her. "Just as if I was a baby again," she said. Her mother smiled. "You *are* a baby – a great big baby."

She knew she had hurt her mother and her father very much by trying to run away. She could tell by their faces, though neither said anything. They both looked older, and sadder. Perhaps she should have let them talk to her first. After all, she might have killed Miss Bradshaw. She looked at the "Get Well" cards on her table – from her school, from Esmé and Joanna and Kathy, and even one from Doreen and Miss Bradshaw – and went on thinking. Freckles *was* too strong for her. Even with the pelham, she knew she couldn't control him. He needed an even stronger bit, which would saw at his mouth, and one of those martingales to keep his head down. She couldn't imagine him shackled like that. The only other solution was to ride him better.

Emma lay and pondered. Was she really a good rider? She had gone to the riding school for a long time, but had she really taken in anything that Miss Bradshaw or Doreen had been trying to teach her – about her seat, and how to use the reins properly, and how to pace a horse, and control it? She had told her mother that the riding school ponies were no good, and that was why she needed her own. Yet other people had managed on riding school ponies much better than she had. They had been chosen for events, while she had been passed over. Why was that?

Many times Miss Bradshaw and Doreen had urged her to concentrate on what she was doing. They had told her parents that she could be a good rider if she really tried. But she had always secretly thought she knew better than they did. She did go off in a dream when she was riding, she knew that. But she didn't want a pony that you manoeuvred around like a motor car. She wanted a special relationship, to be able to ramble with her pony. That was why she wanted Freckles so much. So. She had a special relationship with him. Why, then, did things go wrong so often? Did he let her down or did she let him down? The fact is, Emma told herself, I let him down. I'm not training him properly. I let him do what he wants because it's easier, and often what he wants is the same as what I want. But not always – and that's the trouble.

Her mother came in with beef tea and toast and sat down by her bed. Emma opened her eyes. "Mum," she said, "I've been having a long think."

"And what were you thinking about?"

"About Freckles and me. I've decided I must learn to ride him better."

Her mother's face clouded.

"We'll have a talk about all that when you're quite well," she said. "Dr Cameron's coming this afternoon. If he agrees you'll be able to sit up properly tomorrow, and get up a bit, and have visitors."

"Oh, I hope so. When will my arm be out of plaster?"

"Not for a while yet."

Dr Cameron examined her head, and neck, and eyes.

"You've obeyed orders," he said, "so you can start to move that head around a bit now. But take it very easily, mind."

Emma felt weak and dizzy when she tried to leave her bed, and her left arm hung, a dead weight, at her side. She longed to go outside and visit Freckles, but she had been forbidden to do so. She peered through the landing window for a glimpse of him, couldn't see him in his paddock, and panicked.

"Mum!" she cried, and nearly fell. She caught hold of the banisters with her one good arm and shut her eyes.

The dizziness passed and she found herself looking down at a small, olive-coloured face, framed by two long black pigtails. "Kathy!" she cried. "Whatever are you doing here? Where's Mum?"

Kathy led her back to bed. "I thought I'd come and see you. It's Saturday, you know. Your mum had to go out, and she asked me to stay with you."

"Where's everybody? Where's Peter?"

"Your dad's working, and Peter's out."

"And where's Freckles? What have they done with Freckles while I've been ill?"

"I don't know. I really don't know."

"Anything new happening at school?" Emma asked

after a pause.

"It's all just the same – dead boring. And I'll tell you something else."

"What?"

"I'm getting really tired of going round the town with Esmé and Joanna every Saturday. It frightens me what they get up to, especially Esmé. I'm sure she'll get caught one day. And then we sit in the coffee bar for hours, over one coke. I really loved it that day we came out to watch you at the gymkhana."

"The others couldn't get away fast enough after the fancy dress."

"I know, but I stayed."

"Your parents have got a shop, haven't they?"

"Just a little one – they had a bigger one in Uganda. I

80

help in it sometimes, but I think I'd like to get out into the country more."

"Kathy, what are you trying to say?"

"Well, if I came and helped you at weekends, with Freckles, brushing him, and looking after him, and all that ..."

"Well?"

"If I did that, I wondered ..." Here Kathy paused for a long time.

"Oh, for goodness sake, Kathy, what did you wonder?"

"Well, would you teach me to ride?"

Emma sank back on her pillows. Of course she would! But she had a dreadful feeling inside that Freckles wasn't here any more.

"Oh, Kathy ..." she began. At that moment Peter put his head round the door.

"Stay with Emma," Kathy cried. "I'm just going to make some tea."

When she'd gone Emma looked at Peter. "Peter, you must tell me what's happened to Freckles. I don't think he's here, is he? If I ever try to ask Mum she puts me off. Where is he? I have to know."

She looked up at him with an anxious, drawn face.

"It's been drummed into me that you mustn't be worried until you're quite out of danger. I wish you wouldn't ask me."

"Peter, I have to know."

"If I tell you, you mustn't let on that I have. Promise!"

"I promise."

"Well, then, he's gone back to Mr Riley."

"Gone back to Mr Riley! For good! Oh, Peter, they wouldn't do that! They couldn't!"

Chapter Eleven

Emma's school friends came to visit her one day as she was lying in the orchard on a rug, mourning her lost Freckles. Bodger and Solomon were sitting close by, but Tabitha was nowhere to be seen.

"I think your parents have behaved rottenly," Esmé told her. "I wouldn't have believed it of them."

"After all, it was Freckles who found you," Joanna put in. "He deserves to be given a medal, not sent away."

"And to think I was going to help with him, and learn to ride," Kathy said wistfully.

"Don't know why you're so keen on that idea." Esmé was scornful. "You'd have ended up with concussion, I should think. But we'll have to see what we can do to help Emma."

"Couldn't you try to buy him back?" Joanna asked.

"What with? I've lost all my pocket money until goodness knows when because of that wretched vegetable garden. Anyway Dad would just send him straight back."

"Tackle your mother about it," Joanna advised. "Say you want to go and see him. Then when she sees you with him she might relent. Why don't you do that?"

"Yes, that might be best. When I'm quite better I'll get her to take me."

"Must go, or we'll miss the bus," Esmé said and she and Joanna jumped to their feet.

"I'll stay with you a bit longer, Emma," Kathy told her. "That's if you'd like me to."

Emma and Kathy sat on in the orchard. It was a beautiful June day. The daffodils were over, but at the far end of the orchard where Joe had meant to make hay for Freckles, the grass was long and thick, overtopped by tall stems of cow parsley.

"I expect Dad will cut it all down now," Emma sighed. Then, "Look!", she cried, "Look, Kathy! Can you see what I see? Oh, Tabitha, you've done it at last!"

Tabitha waddled out of the long grass, making a path through it with her large webbed feet, and behind her tumbled one, two, three, four ... fifteen little ducklings, all in a line.

"It is fifteen, isn't it Kathy? I can't believe it. You are clever, Tabitha. I knew you'd do it. I must go and tell Joe. He's in the vegetable garden. I'll be back soon, Tabitha, and bring you some food."

"Don't rush. Remember you've got to take things easy," Kathy called after her. "I'll just go in and telephone my mum or she'll wonder what's happened to me."

Emma sat on an upturned box in the vegetable garden talking to Joe. "You just wait till they get bigger," he was saying. "It won't be long before they do. Sometimes I pity your poor Dad." And he went on digging. "This vegetable garden will never be the same this year, I can tell you that. Potatoes, peas, everything went."

"And no Freckles. I was just thinking of your promise to

make hay for him, and then out of all that long grass walked Tabitha. But you might as well make the hay, because I'll get him back – somehow or other, I'll get him back."

"Is that your dad calling from the house? He doesn't sound too pleased."

"Whatever's the matter now?" Emma rose to her feet and went back through the gate.

She was met by an angry roar from her father. "Emma! Do you know anything about this? That duck is in my pond and it's swarming with ducklings! I thought Joe was meant to collect her eggs. And how has she managed to hatch them anyway?"

Emma ran over to the far side of the lawn, where her father and Joe had made a small pond. Edged with stones and backed on one side by bullrushes and a rose trellis, it was intended for goldfish.

Now it had been annexed by Tabitha, who was trying to instruct her ducklings how to swim.

"She's got fifteen," Emma told him. "I can't believe it."

"So you did know about it then? Where's Joe?"

Joe arrived from the vegetable garden, looking sheepish. "Thought she had some eggs but couldn't find them, sir,"

he said, keeping his eyes off his employer's face.

"It's a conspiracy between the two of you, I can see that. When it comes to animals I can't trust anyone in this house. You're all mad, the lot of you. Get that bird out of my pond at once and don't let her come near it again."

He turned on his heel and marched back into the house.

Joe shook his head. "I'll lose my job on account of you," he said. "We'd better get them back to the orchard. Anyways, very young ones like that can't swim properly – no oil on their feathers. We'd best get them back."

Kathy had returned and the three of them, hindered rather than helped by Bodger, herded Tabitha and her panic-stricken young back across the lawn and towards the

gap in the wire netting that enclosed the orchard. Some got through after Tabitha but many missed the hole and flapped about with their heads stuck in the wire, trying desperately to get to their mother. Kathy picked these ones up and dropped them gently over the fence.

"I'd better get back to my work," Joe said once all the ducklings had been rounded up. "Fill some basins with water and put stones in the bottom. Then they can't drown. And get some saucers of food for them all to keep them occupied."

He went off, and Kathy started to count the ducklings. "Did you say fifteen?" she asked. "I can only count fourteen."

"I'm sure there were fifteen. One must have got stuck at the pond."

They went back to look and found it trapped amongst the stones, bedraggled and half dead, with its head lolling and beak feebly opening and shutting. Emma put it in a little box in the airing cupboard to dry it out. Then she and Kathy went back to block up the holes round the orchard and hunt for bowls and saucers.

It was after tea when Kathy caught the bus home and Emma's mother returned.

"It's a real nuisance having to go in on Saturday," she said. "But I expect you've been managing all right without me."

"You're wrong there." Her husband looked up from his paper. "Emma's somehow persuaded that duck to hatch about a hundred ducklings, and when I came back from the surgery they were all in my pond."

"Emma, really! How many?"

"There were only fifteen, and one's very ill. I must go and look at it."

Emma went to the airing cupboard, and returned sobbing. "It can't be dead, it can't be dead so young." She held the little bundle in her hands.

"Well, there's one less, anyhow," her father said.

"You've still got fourteen, Emma. Surely that's enough? Goodness knows what we're going to do with them. Now take it outside. I must get on with the supper. I'm sorry about it, but it's nothing to make such a fuss about." Her mother gave her a quick kiss and turned back to the stove.

Emma carried the little dead duckling out into the yard and showed it to Joe, who was on his way home.

"Never mind," he said. "Tell you what, I'll make a pond in the orchard for the others, if your father agrees. That will be safer for them."

Later, with Peter holding the torch, she dug a hole for the duckling in the shrubbery, where all the Fairburns' animals were buried. She uprooted a primula from her father's garden and planted it over the grave. Peter wrote on a piece of slate: "Here lies duckling, RIP."

At supper she told her father about Joe's scheme to build a pond in the orchard for the ducks.

"Sometimes I wonder who's employing Joe, you or me," he said mournfully. "I seem to be losing control somehow."

Nelson flew down from the airer on to her father's shoulder and sat there, inspecting his ear. He then climbed on to his head.

"Come on, Nelson, we'll get a little peace and quiet in my study," he said and went out, precariously balancing Nelson, a drink and the evening paper.

"Nelson can always be relied upon to save the day," Peter said. "I suppose I'd better go and do some homework."

"And you'd better get to bed, Emma. It's the first day you've been up for supper."

"Mum, will you come up and see me when I'm in bed? I must talk to you." Emma was suddenly missing Freckles very much. Ducklings were all right, but they weren't the same. She must see him soon, or she didn't know what she would do.

Chapter Twelve

Emma lay in bed, worrying. What was she going to say to her mother? At one time she would have cried, and stamped her foot, and demanded that they get Freckles back from Mr Riley. Now she did not know what to do. She felt trapped by her own action. If she had not rushed off at night like that she would not have had an accident, and then they might not have sent Freckles away. They were being very kind to her, but they never mentioned him. It was as if he had never existed. And Peter wouldn't help. He had told her he thought she was better off without a pony. Only Joe seemed to know how she felt. One day, when she was sitting in the empty stable, as she often did now, he came into the paddock to pull up the ragwort before it seeded. The grass was growing fast too, and thistles and lots of little wild flowers were shooting up, now Freckles was not there to eat and trample them all down.

"If I were you I wouldn't mope," he had said. "I'd do something."

"What can I do?" she remembered answering.

"Ask your mother to take you to see him," he had told her. "I know your dad would be against it, but I think *she*'ll know how you've been feeling. And after that you never know. I'll pull up the ragwort just in case." He had turned round and smiled at her. She lay back on the pillow, thinking about what he had said, as she waited for her cocoa.

Her mother came into the room, carrying two mugs. "I thought I'd have some with you," she said, sitting down on the bed. "Now, what did you want to talk to me about?"

"You can guess, can't you?"

"Is it about Freckles?"

"Mum, I want to see him. I must see him. You and Dad are being very nice to me, but I'm so unhappy."

"Do you think seeing him would do any good? I feel it would only upset you. Your father won't have him back – it's no use talking to him about it. And I'm sure Freckles is happy with Mr Riley. That's why we let him go back there."

"But I *want* to see him. I keep thinking about him and wondering how he is. If I found out he was really happy without me I might get used to not having him."

"You're going back to school tomorrow, and you've missed quite a lot. You must do some work, you know. We don't want to have any more worries with you. And I've got a lot on this week."

"We could go at the weekend – on Sunday, when Mr Riley won't be at market. Oh, Mum, do please ring up and find out. Please!"

"Well, if you promise to behave when you get there. I don't want any scenes."

"I'll try. I might have a ride and then come home. If only I could have a ride sometimes, and talk to him. Please, Mum!"

"Well, I'll ring in the morning. But you do see why we

couldn't keep him, don't you? He was too strong for you – it was dangerous."

"The funny thing is, while I was lying in bed all that time, I was thinking about Freckles and me. And do you know, just before I found out that he wasn't with us any more, Kathy asked me to give her riding lessons. Think of that!"

"I'm not sure you could teach riding."

"Of course I could! You think I can't ride at all, don't you? What about the rosettes Freckles won? Look at them over there, on my dressing table. And I haven't even got a photograph of him …"

Emma realised she was starting to shout. Suddenly she looked at her mother, who was sitting very still. She knew what her mother must be thinking: "If Freckles came back it would start all over again. There'd be another accident, this time with Kathy. It could be worse next time …"

She wriggled down the bed and put her arms round her mother's neck. "Oh, Mum, I know I worried you. Really, I know inside I must learn to ride better. That's what I'd been thinking when I had to lie still all that time. Mostly it was my fault that things went wrong. I thought I didn't need to learn anything more about riding. And now I've lost Freckles."

"Don't cry." Her mother hugged her. "I'll telephone Mr Riley in the morning and see if we can go over on Sunday. But you mustn't make a scene."

And with that promise Emma had to be content.

It seemed strange to be catching the bus for school again, but everyone welcomed her when she arrived, and Miss Blake was kind, except that she gave her some special work to help her catch up.

Emma only half attended to her lessons, she was so anxious to know if her mother had telephoned Mr Riley, and whether they would be seeing Freckles on Sunday. She rushed home after school instead of going to the shop to buy sweets with her friends as she usually did.

"I can't get him," her mother told her. "The telephone seems to be out of order."

Emma's face fell.

"But we'll go on Sunday in any case," her mother added. "He's sure to be there."

For the rest of the week she was dreaming of Sunday, and when at last they set off, in her mother's little red car, she kept urging her to drive faster.

"It's a very twisty road," said her mother. "We don't want an accident. I'll have to be careful going up that hill. You know how rutted the track was before. Look out for the turning, will you?"

Emma looked contentedly about her. The trees were in full leaf now and it was all much greener than when they had come before. They were on a high road and through the trees she caught glimpses of the river winding below them. Beyond the river and the fields stretched the open moors, purple now with heather.

"It's so beautiful," she murmured. "I'd like to live here. Perhaps I could go and live with Mr and Mrs Riley, as a stable girl ..."

"Don't be silly," said her mother. "Look out for the turning."

"There it is," cried Emma.

They turned up the track that led to Mr Riley's farm. It seemed more overgrown than before and had deep potholes in it now.

"There's the farmhouse, I can see it," cried Emma. "Pull into the yard, Mum. Let me out, please let me out!"

Emma jumped out and ran towards the farmhouse and rang the bell. Then she hammered on the door. But there was no answer. She looked round.

Her mother was inspecting the yard and the outhouses.

"There doesn't seem to be anyone here," she said uncertainly. "I wonder where they all are."

"No animals – no nothing. What's happened? Where's Freckles? Oh, Mum, where have they taken Freckles?"

"I don't know. Perhaps they're on holiday."

"They'd have left someone here, you know they would. Someone should be here."

She tried to peer through the farmhouse windows, but all the curtains were drawn. Then she went to inspect the field where she had first met Freckles. There was horse manure scattered about, and it wasn't very old.

"I don't think he's been gone long," she said. "Oh, what can have happened to him?"

"I think we'd better go to the village at the bottom of the hill and ask," her mother decided. "We can get tea there. I could do with a cup."

They climbed back into the car and set off down the hill again, turning left at the bottom and stopping in the village. Here, they made for a cottage selling teas.

Settled at a corner table, Emma's mother asked the landlady about Mr Riley and described the farm up on the hill.

"That was a bad business," the woman said. "It was so sudden, took everyone by surprise. One minute there he was, large as life, telling his stories and running his farm, and the next ..."

"What happened to him?"

"The next minute he was dead – dropped dead at the wheel of his car. He'd just got back from market. Heart attack, it was. She found him there, poor woman. He'd been complaining of chest pain, it appears, but thought nothing of it. Thought it was indigestion. 'You're feeding me too well, old lady,' he'd say, and they'd both laugh."

"Didn't he see a doctor?"

"Didn't believe in doctors, neither of them did."

"What happened to Mrs Riley?"

"And the pony that was there, the brown and white one, what happened to him?" broke in Emma.

"All sold, sold at auction. Mrs Riley was taken off by relatives. Farm's to be sold, I believe. A bad business, and so sudden. Why, what's the matter with the little girl? Don't take on so. He was a good man, nothing to worry about, and Mrs Riley'll be back in Devonshire: she'll be looked after. Whatever is the matter?"

"It's the pony, Freckles. He was her pony. You don't know where he's gone?"

"I don't, no. He went to a large auction, I believe. I don't know who bought him. But I'm sure he'll be all right. If he was a good pony he'll be all right. It's only the wild ones that go for horsemeat …"

Here Emma burst into great sobs. Her mother put her arm round her shoulders, thanked the landlady for the tea, and led her back to the car.

"Well, I couldn't help it, Emma," she said, after a long pause, while Emma sat hunched and silent in the seat next to her. "How was I to know that would happen? Freckles seemed happy to see Mr Riley when he came to fetch him, and he promised me he wouldn't sell him. How was I to know?"

"Even if it was my fault, you shouldn't have let him go. You shouldn't. It was mean of you – it was cruel. I'll never see him again now, never." She started to cry again.

"Emma, please don't be so upset. I'll talk to your father. We'll get you another pony. Please, Emma!"

"I don't want another pony. Can't you understand that? Can't either of you understand that? I only want Freckles, and now he's gone for good, and I'll never see him again. You shouldn't have sent him away. You know you shouldn't. I don't want to speak to you again, ever."

Her mother started the car and drove slowly home.

Chapter Thirteen

"**I**t's no good. I can't hate them, however much I try."
Emma was sitting with her friends under a tree in
the playground, waiting for the bell to ring.

"I'm sick of hearing about your troubles with your
parents," Esmé broke in. "You go on and on about how
awful your father is, and how much you miss Freckles.
They've offered to get you another pony; why won't you
agree to that?"

"Because I won't, that's why. I can't expect *you* to
understand. And if you won't let me talk about it I don't
want to be friends with you."

"I'm fed up with you moaning, too," Joanna got up and
pulled Esmé to her feet. "Let's go in now, the bell's gone."

Kathy stayed behind.

"I know how you feel," she said. "As if your whole
world's fallen apart. My parents felt like that too, when
they had to leave Uganda. But theirs has mended, and
yours will."

"Don't know about that. I feel so hopeless."

"Late in again," said Miss Blake, "I don't know what's come over you, Emma. You'd better pull yourself together. You're near the bottom now in the tests."

Emma hardly heard her. Where could Freckles be? Peter had promised to try to find out, but he was busy with A level exams. The worst might have happened: he might not have been given a character at the auction, and no one would buy a pony without a character except very cheaply. And if he had been bought cheaply he might have been sent off to Belgium to be made into horsemeat. She had seen a headline about it the other day, and read the article – about New Forest ponies, packed off there, without food or water, unable to move around. It didn't bear thinking about. She stared into space until it was time to go home.

"Miss Blake telephoned me," her mother told her when she arrived back.

"Whatever for?"

"She says you're not attending at school. You may have to be kept down next term. Then you'd lose your friends, wouldn't you? They'd be going on to the Comprehensive without you."

"I can't help it. I don't like them anyway, except for Kathy."

Emma went out listlessly to inspect the ducklings.

Peter, who had just come in, followed her out.

"Good news!" he told her. "I've discovered where Freckles is."

"Oh! Where, Peter. Where?"

"It's a riding school, at Eastcot, the other side of town. The school's owned by a Captain Wetherby."

"Freckles! In a riding school! I can't imagine it!"

"Get Mum to take you to see him: it'll put you out of your misery. Better come in to tea now."

Emma danced into the house. At least he was alive, at least she knew where he was. Now she could work on trying to get him back again.

"Well," her mother said, turning round from the stove, "you look cheerful, for once. What's happened?"

"Peter's found out where Freckles is, so please, please, will you take me to see him?"

"Is that true, Peter?"

"I've found out who bought him, anyway."

"It's a riding school, Mum. I could go and book a ride on him. I could see if they're looking after him, and if he's happy. Oh, please, Mum. Let's go on Saturday."

"I really think you should go," Peter advised. "I'm tired of dealing with those ducks every night whilst Emma just moons about. Get her back on course, Mum, for goodness sake."

"Who's going where?" her father, who had just come in, wanted to know.

"We've found out where Freckles is, and we're going to see him, at least Emma and I are," his wife told him firmly.

"He's not to come back here, is that understood?"

"Of course."

"Not by me," Emma muttered, and Peter winked at her.

It took over an hour to get to Eastcot. The school was situated outside the town, its entrance barred by great wooden gates.

"Doesn't look very inviting," Alison said. "No bell or anything. How do we make them hear?"

"There's a bungalow at the side. Let's ask there."

A frightened-looking little woman came to the door wearing carpet slippers on her feet.

"My daughter has come to see about a ride," Alison explained. "Is Captain Wetherby in?"

"He only sees people by appointment." The woman looked nervously over her shoulder.

"We've come quite a long way. If he's around I would like to see him."

"Wait in here. I'll go and see." She ushered them into a small sitting room and left them there.

Emma looked round the room. "Look at those great antlers over the fireplace," she said.

"I don't like this room," Alison replied. She was sitting on the edge of the hard leather sofa, while Emma perched on a high-backed chair.

"And look at the little fox curled up in front of the fireplace," Emma cried. "Poor little thing. Do you think Captain Wetherby shot him and had him stuffed? And there are two more here, dressed in little hunting jackets and riding boots."

"It's a bearskin rug, too," said her mother. "I don't like all these trophies. And look at the guns on the walls. It gives me the creeps."

"What do you want?" The voice came from behind them.

Emma's mother spun round. "Captain Wetherby?" she asked.

"Who else would I be?"

The voice was bullying, harsh, and the man's appearance matched his voice. He was large and florid, with dark hair greased and brushed back on either side of a straight, white parting. He was dressed in riding breeches, an open-necked shirt and hacking jacket. As he spoke he tapped a riding crop against his leg.

"What do you want?" he repeated. "Mrs Wetherby has already told you that I only see people by appointment."

"Emma, my daughter, wanted to fix up a ride."

"It's a residential school. We don't have casual rides here."

"She wanted a ride on a pony we once owned." Emma's mother went on to describe Freckles.

"Well she can't. That particular pony's out on a ride now."

"Can we see round the school then? We may want to come another day."

"I've told you, no casual rides. And as for that pony you're talking about, I've had enough trouble getting him to my liking without your daughter butting in. No, you can't see round. It's not convenient just now."

"Please, please, when can I see Freckles?" Emma spoke for the first time.

"No reason for you to see him at all. I'll bid you good day now. Martha, show this lady out."

He strode out of the room, and through the open door Emma and her mother heard him shouting at his wife for letting them in.

"Well," said Alison, "what do you make of that?"

"He's a horrible man, a perfectly horrible man." Emma was in tears.

"You can't run a riding school and not let people come for rides," said her mother. "There's something very odd about all this. Looks to me as if he's got something to hide."

"Poor Freckles! With that man! We must do something, Mum."

"Well, we can't do anything now, except go home. I didn't like the look of that riding crop, though, I must say."

Chapter Fourteen

At supper that night Emma's father and Peter heard the full story of the visit to the riding school.

"You never saw such a man, honestly, Jim," Alison told her husband. "So boorish and rude."

"Perhaps he's good with horses, but not with people," he replied.

"Why wouldn't he let Emma and me in, then, just to look round?"

"You hadn't telephoned for an appointment, had you? You just turned up out of the blue? I refuse to see patients when they do that to me. If he doesn't want children to have casual rides on his ponies I don't see why he should immediately be branded as a horse molester."

"He may be all right." Alison didn't sound convinced. "But I thought his attitude was most odd. I'd like to find out more about him and his riding school."

"And about Freckles," Emma put in.

"As I discovered where he was, I'd better try to learn

more about this Captain Wetherby." Peter got up from the table. "Leave it to me, the great amateur sleuth. We don't want little Carrots having a nervous breakdown."

"Just off, sir," said Joe, appearing at the kitchen door. He was making strange gestures towards the yard with his hands.

Emma's father looked at him in surprise. "Not got St Vitus's dance, have you?" he asked.

"No, sir, just going." He went out, looking back over his shoulder at Emma as he did so. She followed him out.

"The pond!" he whispered. "They're in the pond again.

Can't stop now." He got on his bicycle and rode away.

"Peter!"

"What's up?"

"Come out here a minute."

Together they manoeuvred Tabitha and her ducklings back into the orchard and repaired as best they could the damage she had done.

"Dad's sure to notice in the morning," Peter said. "We must build that pond in the orchard. I'll get Alan and some of the others over at the weekend, and Joe can help."

"Dad said he could only do it in his own time."

"Well, I've got a tenner I can give him."

"Peter! However did you get hold of that?"

"Won it on a horse."

"They won't let you in to a bookmaker's, will they?"

Peter just grinned. "Anyway, don't worry," he said. "I'll find out about Freckles now that we know where he is. You've got to do some work, though. That'll keep the parents happy."

On Saturday Peter rounded up Alan and Brian and Neil to help make the new pond. With them came another boy Emma didn't know.

"This is Steve," Peter told her. "He lives over Eastcot way, so I started my enquiries with him. He's just left school and wanted a job, and do you know where he's landed one?"

"No! Where?"

"Tell her, Steve."

"At that riding school Peter was on about. Captain Wetherby's taken me on as a stable hand. Rotten pay – I'm not going to stay long."

"What's it like, the riding school?"

"Well, to tell you the honest truth, it's terrible. He's got a big mortgage on it, I think. It hasn't been going long, and from what his wife tells me he's at his wit's end to make it pay."

"Why's it terrible?"

"He's short of money, that's why it's terrible. He takes these children for the holidays, boards them but makes them do all the work, and feeds them as cheaply as he can. He advertises for them: they're none of them local children. It's my opinion the parents want to get shot of them."

"I'll have to think about this," muttered Emma.

Joe trundled his bicycle in through the gate, balancing on it some waterproof cement he'd promised to bring. Alan and Peter climbed the steps into the yard to help him bring it down into the orchard.

"Now we can begin," Peter said.

Joe wiped his forehead. "Heavy, that was," he groaned. "I don't know why I'm doing all this for you, on my day off."

Peter pushed a five pound note into his hand and closed his fist over it. Immediately Joe's face broke into a broad grin.

"And I'll get you some orange juice with ice in it," cried Emma. She hurried indoors.

Under Joe's direction the hole was dug, the concrete mixed and spread, and finally covered so that Tabitha and her fourteen ducklings could not get in and spoil it.

"Should be fine by tomorrow," Joe told them. "You've got seven ducks and seven drakes there by the look of it. They'll be ready for the pot by Christmas, I should say."

"They will not go in the pot!" Emma was outraged.

"What are you going to do with them then?"

'Find homes for them, and keep one little duck as a friend for Tabitha."

"You'll be lucky! I'll be off now. Thank you for the fiver. Any news of Freckles?"

"What'll you do then?" he asked after Emma had told

him of the visit to Captain Wetherby.

"Rescue him, of course."

Joe shook his head. "Mind you keep on the right side of the law," he told her. "Could be the last straw if your father had to bail you out. I can't see that pony coming back here, but you never know. I'll make the hay just in case."

Emma hugged him, and then waved as he pushed his bicycle out of the gate.

"Seriously," said Peter as they sat in the orchard together, contemplating Tabitha trying without success to get into the new pond. "What are we going to do about Freckles? What do you suggest, Steve?"

Steve took some time to answer. Then he said, "I don't mind telling you, I'm a bit scared of that man. I wouldn't want to get on the wrong side of him. But when I think of that pony ... I don't think he can take much more."

"Couldn't you just quietly ride him away, when Captain Wetherby wasn't looking? We'd hide him somewhere, if you did."

"That man's got eyes in the back of his head, and I wouldn't trust his wife. Those big gates are always kept shut. If I opened them he'd know something was up. The only hope is for him to escape by himself."

"How could he do that, if he was shut in a stable?"

"I see to them last thing at night. I could leave his stable door unlocked and hope they wouldn't notice. Then it's my job to make sure the big gates are secure. I could take down the bar, then come back at first light and push them open a bit. Then it would be up to Freckles."

"Then you could be waiting and catch him as he came through, couldn't you?" Emma was breathless with excitement. "What do you think, Peter?"

"There are so many 'ifs'," said Peter. "*If* the stable door was ajar, *if* Freckles noticed, *if* he got into the yard without Captain Wetherby seeing or hearing, *if* he managed to push through the big gates, *if* ..."

"Oh, I know all that, but he's so clever, he'd probably manage it if he got the chance," Emma said proudly.

"I know he's chewed through his halter twice, and pushed up the bolt on his stable. It's tied down now with cord. He's been punished for that."

"There, you see. I'm sure he'd manage it, if he was given a chance. Let's try it."

"You'll have to find somewhere to hide him first. Captain Wetherby'll be after him! He's valuable property – the right size, and everything, I've often heard him say so."

"I'll find somewhere. I'll ask at school. Please do it, Steve."

"Next Friday would be a good time. A lot of children arrive on Saturday for the holidays, so the day before would be quiet. And I heard Captain Wetherby was driving off to get some of them and wouldn't be back until next day. That would be the best time."

"We'll do it then – Friday night. I'll let Peter know where he's to go."

"What are you lot plotting?" Alison had come out of the house with a plate of buns and some lemonade. "I'm not going to do any more Saturday shifts. It's too tiring." She sank down on the grass beside them.

"Plotting! What makes you think we're plotting?"

"Well, I hope it's nothing too dreadful, that's all. And by the way, that duck's in your new pond."

In the resulting uproar Steve left. Peter saw him to the gate. Watching him go, Emma felt she could trust him to carry out his part in the plan. Now she had to carry out hers: she must find a place to hide Freckles.

Chapter Fifteen

"**L**et's be friends again."

Emma couldn't stand it any longer. Here she was, sitting with Kathy on one side of their favourite tree, and Esmé and Joanna, not talking to them, were on the other. It had been the same all through lessons.

"Please, let's be friends. I've got something very important to tell you." Swallowing her pride, Emma crawled round the tree and sat next to Esmé, who turned her back to her.

"Don't see why I should."

"Oh, please," said Kathy, who had followed Emma.

"I won't keep on and on about Freckles, only …"

"There, you see, you're starting again already."

"But this is different. I feel better now. I know where he is, and we've all got to help him."

"I tell you, I don't want anything to do with it. We've enough troubles of our own, at home."

"Wait till you hear. Can I tell you?"

"Oh, all right. But hurry up."

"I can't tell you when you've got your back to me."

"Let's go over in the sun," Kathy suggested. "It's cold here. Let's go and sit on that wall over there."

The playground had asphalt in the centre for games, surrounded by trees and grass. On one side a low wall divided it from the car and bicycle park, and it was towards this that the four made their way.

As they sat side by side on the wall, Emma recounted her visit to Captain Wetherby and what Steve had told them about the riding school.

"So you see," she ended, "We must get him out. Steve's too scared to do it himself, but he's going to give Freckles a chance to escape on his own. If he does, though, we've got to have somewhere to hide him. That's why I thought I'd

ask you all. Do you know anywhere where we could keep him?"

"Don't see why we should. You can't hide a horse in a town." Joanna was scornful.

"There might be land that isn't used, or a shed somewhere. Round us he'd be noticed right away. It must be where people wouldn't expect to find him."

Esmé, who until then had been swinging her legs up and down, jumping on and off the wall, and showing every sign of wanting to get away, suddenly went quite still. "Did you say a shed?" she asked. "My dad's got a shed."

"Where?"

"You know he works on the railways. Well, he's got a piece of land they let him have, on the railway side, but it's really on wasteland, in the middle of nowhere; he's supposed to grow vegetables on it, but he never goes near it. And there's quite a big shed there. I don't know what he keeps in it."

"How do you get there?"

"You go along a track through a coal yard at the back of the station, and over a little bridge. It's all wild and overgrown. The branch line to Marston used to run along there, but it's been closed for ages. I went with Dad once, before he started to go to pubs all the time. I could take you there if you wanted me to."

"Freckles' escape is fixed for Friday night. We haven't got long."

"We break up Thursday," Joanna put in. "Surely you lot haven't forgotten that."

"Then we'll have all Friday to get ready," Kathy cried. "Where shall we meet?"

"Could we go on our bikes?" Emma suggested. "All meet with our bikes at our house and say we're going on an expedition? I could get Mum to make sandwiches for us, then we could stay out all day. Is it too far to cycle?"

"Not really." Esmé was in charge now. "Not if we go

cross-country. We'll all meet at your house at ten o'clock, Friday. I'll bring coke. I've collected quite a lot." She looked at the others, but Emma pretended not to hear. "And Kathy, you can bring some sweets and chocolate from your shop. What will you bring, Joanna?"

Joanna sat and thought. "I'll just bring myself," she said at last.

"It sounds perfect." Emma looked round contentedly, "That is, providing we can get him there. I knew you'd help me."

Two days later the four of them were sitting on some upturned boxes in the sunshine, munching. Their cycles lay on the ground beside them.

"Your mother makes really good sandwiches, I'll say that for her," Esmé told Emma.

"This place looks really decrepit, now that we've arrived," Joanna said.

"All the better. No one will think of looking for him here. We'd better make sure he can't get out, though." Emma looked round.

The track which had once been a railway line ran along one side of the plot of land where they were sitting. The rails had been removed and it was now overgrown with wild roses, brambles and grass. A stout fence ran along the top of the cutting.

"That's useful!" she said. "Freckles won't be able to get out that way, at any rate."

The other three sides of the plot consisted of waste ground, knee deep in docks and thistles and cow parsley. Beyond that Emma could make out the flags on the golf course, and beyond that, although she could not see it, stood her parents' house.

"Has it always been waste ground?" she asked Esmé. "It seems a shame that it's so overgrown."

"There used to be allotments here for the railway

workers," Esmé told her. "When the branch line was running they were dropped off at the halt there, with their tools and everything. But since the line finished nobody's bothered with them. Don't know why my dad kept his on. What are you doing, Kathy?"

Kathy had found an old broom and was in the shed sweeping vigorously, stirring up great clouds of dust. "I like housework," she cried. "I really do."

"Stop it!" Emma was sneezing. "We don't want the shed too clean. Freckles will make a terrible mess of it. Some of the boxes will do for his hay and carrots. We can put all this old straw on the floor for him, and keep the fork and spade and wheelbarrow on one side to clear out the manure. There'll be plenty of that, I can tell you."

"Is that what he's going to eat, then, hay and carrots?" Joanna asked.

"Mostly, and some pony nuts, but we mustn't give him many or they'll make him too frisky. Joe's making hay in the orchard and it'll be ready this weekend. I'll bring as much as I can over on my bicycle. We'll have to clear those shelves and store it up there, so that he can't get at it all at once. I've been collecting carrots too. I take half of whatever Mum buys. Luckily she thinks they're good for you and is always getting them."

"Let's go outside and see to the fence." Esmé took Emma by the hand. She was enjoying this adventure. They were really friends again now. "You look around, Joanna, and see if you can find any string, or nails or a hammer."

They found sagging barbed wire round the allotment, most of it lying on the ground and overgrown with grass and weeds. It was difficult to pull up, but at last they had it fixed to the few remaining posts.

"It won't take Freckles long to eat all this," Emma observed as she inspected the matted rows of bolting lettuces and cauliflowers which were struggling through the weeds. "He got through everything in Dad's vegetable garden in record time. I hope Joe manages to make a lot of hay."

"Anyway we can lock him in at night. There's a bolt on the door," Joanna said. "I mended that when I found the nails."

"We'll have to take turns keeping an eye on him in the daytime, though."

"What are our parents going to say when we spend so much time away from home?" Esmé wanted to know.

"You'll have to pretend you're coming to help me in the shop in the holidays," Kathy said as she came out of the shed with her broom.

"And what will you pretend, then?" asked Esmé.

"Oh, I don't know. Come and look at the shed."

They stepped inside and found it spotless. Even the window had been wiped clean of dust and cobwebs.

"Oh, Kathy, really." Emma hugged her. "All we have to do now is work out a rota for keeping watch during the day, so that we can hide him if anyone comes."

"Well, I'm exhausted already. I don't know what we've let ourselves in for. Anyway, let's drink to Freckles and good luck!" Esmé handed everyone a tin. "And now for home." Then she looked round. "How do we get our bikes out?" she asked.

"You've wired us in," Kathy cried.

"Wait a minute." Joanna went back into the shed. "I put some hooks on a shelf here. We can hammer them into a post and hook the wire round. Then we can get in and out easily."

Once they'd constructed their makeshift door, they all set off for home, Emma going her way and the others theirs.

"Ring me on Saturday," called Emma. "I hope I'll have good news for you."

Chapter Sixteen

"Who can that be? You're not on call." Alison rolled over and picked up the telephone by the bed. It was barely light.

"Some idiot probably thinks I am."

"It's Steve, for Peter," she said. "I suppose I'd better tell him. He can take the call in the hall."

She woke Peter with some difficulty and he stumbled sleepily downstairs.

Emma, who had hardly slept all night for worrying, heard Peter go down and followed him.

"Keep quiet or I won't be able to concentrate," he muttered. He was listening intently.

"I suppose you can't do any more," Peter said at last. "You'd better go home and ... Blast. His money's run out." He turned to Emma. "Freckles did come through the gates ..."

"I knew he would, I knew he'd escape."

"Steve was waiting, with a halter and sugar lumps to catch him, but ..."

"But what?"

"Freckles just went straight past him. He broke into a trot when Steve ran after him. Steve lost sight of him, and he doesn't know where he is now."

"Oh, my goodness!"

"We can't do anything. We don't know where he is. Someone's bound to find him and report it to the police."

"They might not. They might just keep him. Or they might return him to Captain Wetherby. Oh, Peter, what shall we do?"

"Nothing. We can't do anything. I'm going to have some breakfast."

A very despondent Emma followed him into the kitchen.

"Cheer up," squawked Nelson.

"Oh, shut up."

"Time for tea, cocky."

"Nelson, if you don't keep quiet ..."

"What is the matter?" asked her mother, coming into the kitchen in her dressing gown. "You both look very glum."

"Nothing, nothing at all. Emma just got up too early. Doesn't agree with her."

"What did Steve want so early?"

"Just wanted to talk, nothing important."

"You're both hiding something, but I expect I'll find out what it is soon enough."

"Coffee! I must have some coffee." Emma's father had come in. He hadn't shaved, and Emma could tell that his temper wasn't good.

"Thought I might as well get up," he said. "That telephone call spoiled my only chance of a good sleep."

"Cheer up," cried Nelson.

Just then the telephone rang again.

"I'll answer it," called Peter, but Alison got there first.

She was outside talking for quite a long while.

"I wonder if you two know anything about this," she said when she came back.

"About what?"

"About Freckles."

"Oh, where is he? What's happened? Is he all right?" Emma's fists were clenched and her eyes wide with fear.

"Of course he's all right. He's at the riding school, where he belongs," said her father, buttering his toast and opening the paper, which had just arrived.

"No, he's not at the riding school, he's at the police station, in the dog pound," said his wife. "Keep calm. I'll give you your coffee now."

Peter's mouth had fallen open.

"At the police station? Do you mean our local one?"

"Yes. It appears that he was trotting along, all by himself, early this morning, when he went through a red traffic light and nearly collided with a van. The van driver caught him and took him to the police station. Sergeant Crane recognised him as the pony that once belonged to us and telephoned me. He's in the dog pound because they've nowhere else to put him, and making a great nuisance of himself. They want us to fetch him right away."

"I knew it. I knew if he had a chance he'd find his way home." Emma was dancing round the kitchen, and Nelson was beating time with a twig he had picked up. Bodger, sensing the excitement, started to bark.

"Stop all that noise," said her father. "So you knew he'd got out. How did you know? What have you been doing behind my back? Whatever it was, we're not keeping him, if that's what you think. He's not our pony now. Just remember that."

"Mum, I must get him. Mum, please take me right away in the car. I'll take the old saddle and bridle, and ..."

"And your hat. Don't forget your hat. All right, we'd better get him, and then work out what to do afterwards."

"He's going back," Emma's father shouted after them.

116

"He's not staying here."

"I'd better go and telephone Steve." Peter followed them out. "He'll be relieved that no harm has come to him."

"Don't let him tell Captain Wetherby he's here," Emma implored him. "Dad might relent, you never know."

When they got to the police station they found Freckles moving restlessly round and round, his head lowered to the ground. The one frightened mongrel in the pound had retreated to the farthest corner of its kennel.

"He keeps going round with his back to the wall," said the sergeant. "Looks as if he's frightened he'll be hit."

"I hardly recognise him," cried Emma. "He's so thin. Look, all his ribs are showing."

She went over to him. He whinnied, but kept his head down. Emma knelt down and put her face against his. She breathed deep into his nose, and at last he did the same to her. His ears came up. For a moment he was the old Freckles. Then he lowered his head again.

"Come and feel, Mum," Emma cried. "His mouth's sore this side. And look. One eye's half closed. And his back has great scars on it."

"I'll fetch a bit of blanket from the cells," said the sergeant. "That way he won't feel the saddle so much. He's nothing but a nuisance here. I'd be glad if you'd take him home with you. We can always contact you if we need to. I take it you'll agree to do that."

"Of course!" Emma said, without waiting for her mother's reply. She bent down to examine his feet. "No one's trimmed his hooves, and his shoes don't fit properly. Oh, Mum, what have they done to him?" She was almost crying.

"He's certainly in a bad state, but I don't know what your father will say when we take him home."

"I don't care what he says. He's not going back to that awful place."

Her mother sighed.

The sergeant returned with a piece of blanket to put on Freckles' back. He whickered with pain as the saddle was adjusted and the girths were pulled tight, and again when the bit caught his sore mouth.

"I'll ride him very gently," called Emma as she set off. "Thank you very much for looking after him."

"By the way," said Sergeant Crane as he saw her mother to her car, "a young reporter saw him when he came to ask about a prisoner and wanted to know what he was doing here. Thought it could make a story for his paper. I told him to go round and see you."

"Well, it is quite a story." Alison sighed again. "And we don't know the end of it yet."

Emma's father and Peter were both out when she arrived back, but Joe, who was working in the garden, came over and helped her.

"Somehow I knew he'd be back," he said. "I'll make the hay for you soon if this weather holds. You'd best get a vet for those sores and a blacksmith for his feet. I doubt if your father will send him back when he sees him."

Emma heard her father's car draw up.

Her father came through into the yard and stopped short when he saw Freckles. "I told you ..." he began.

"Just come and look at him." Emma went over and took him by the hand. "Then you'll understand."

Freckles cowered back at the sight of her father and lowered his head.

"Because you're a man, he's afraid you'll hit him," Emma cried. "Just look at how he's been treated. Those sores on his back have been made by nails on a bad saddle. Joe said we should get a vet, and we need a blacksmith."

"And I'll have to pay for it all, when he doesn't even belong to us."

Then he put out his hand and touched Freckles' head. "Poor little beggar." His voice softened. "I expect he brought it all on himself, but he can stay here for a bit. It'll probably take that man a while to trace us if you didn't give him our address."

"Luckily I didn't." Alison had come up. "I was going to, but he pushed us out before I could."

Kathy telephoned to find out what had happened.

"Everything's fine," Emma told her. "Freckles is back here, so let Esmé and Joanna know we don't need our plan any more. I'll tell you when you can come and start riding lessons. He's so quiet and well behaved at the moment. Not like himself. You won't have any trouble."

It took care and patience, but Emma was on holiday and could devote all her time to getting Freckles well again. Gradually he regained his courage and his spirits, and his wounds healed. She took him for gentle rides round the countryside and one day, passing Mr Giles' farm, remembered the battery hens.

"What are you doing about those poor caged hens?" she asked Peter that evening.

"All under control, dear Carrots," he replied.

"If you call me that again ..."

"Quiet, you two," called her mother. "What are you planning now?"

"Nothing! Nothing! Come into the garden, Emma, for a moment."

"The Animal Rights Brigade are making plans to free them," he told her. "But they want a sketch of the layout of the farm and the sheds. We'll go round this evening just before dark and make one. They said it wouldn't be long now."

"Oh, thanks, Peter. And everything's going well with Freckles. Wouldn't it be wonderful if Captain Wetherby'd given him up for lost, so we could have him back for good!"

"I wouldn't bet on it, if I were you."

"I am rather worried, Mum," Emma said that evening at supper. "He's too good. I wonder if we'll ever get back the old Freckles."

"He's better the way he is," said her father. "That man may have overdone it, but a little discipline never hurts."

Just then the telephone rang.

Her father came back from answering it very red in the face. "I've never been spoken to like that in my life," he roared. "Who does he think he is?"

"What are you talking about?"

"That Captain Wetherby. He wants the pony back. He's coming for him with a box on Sunday."

"That's the day after tomorrow," cried Emma. "Oh, Dad, you can't let him go!"

"There's no help for it. He's not ours now. The man was so rude that against my better judgment I did offer to buy him back, but he wouldn't hear of it. No, I'm afraid he's got to go."

"Emma, aren't you going to finish your supper?" called her mother.

"Don't want any more." Emma had gone out to the paddock. She needed to think. The plan must be put into operation, and there was no time to be lost.

Chapter Seventeen

How could she get to the telephone without her mother or father overhearing, and wanting to know what she was doing? That was the problem. She must get hold of Esmé and tell her what had happened. She would have to bring the others because they would need to move hay, and straw, and carrots, and of course Freckles himself, over to the shed without anyone noticing. How was it to be done? She didn't even want Peter to know where Freckles was hidden. Her father had said something about Steve giving their address away to Captain Wetherby. Perhaps he had been bullied and forced into it. Perhaps Peter might be kidnapped and hurt too because he was Steve's friend. Emma knew she was being silly but she couldn't help it. Captain Wetherby was a nightmare figure to her, capable of anything. What could she do?

"Esmé for you on the telephone," shouted her mother over the wall. "Hurry up. I've told her to hold on."

Emma rushed back into the house from the paddock.

"Esmé," she gasped. "I'm so pleased to hear from you."

"Well, that's a change," said Esmé. "It's always Kathy this and Kathy that now. I thought you'd quite forgotten me."

"No, I hadn't. And Esmé —" She put her hand round the receiver and whispered, "Danger."

"What?" said Esmé. "Speak up. This line's not very good."

"Can't. Danger!"

"What are you talking about? I wish you'd speak up."

"Can't. They'll hear. Oh, Esmé! He's coming. For you know who."

"But Kathy rang and told me ..."

"I know, but it's all changed. We've got to put it into operation, you know, the Plan."

"What plan?"

"Oh, for goodness sake, Esmé, your plan, *you* know."

"Are you going to be much longer on that telephone?" asked her father, putting his head round the door. "I've an urgent call to make."

"Not much longer. Esmé, have you got it?"

There was a pause, and then Esmé's voice: "I've got it. What do you want me to do?"

Emma was almost crying with relief. "Be there with the others, with provisions, anything, ten o'clock tomorrow."

"What provisions?"

"Oh, anything, biscuits, nuts, anything."

"Nuts. Why ever do you want nuts?"

"Emma, will you get off that telephone." Her father was really angry now.

"Goodbye. I'll be seeing you then."

She couldn't do any more. If they didn't help her, it was the end.

The doorbell rang and she went to answer it. Two young men stood there, one with a notebook in his hand, the other with a camera.

"We're from the local paper," the one with the notebook told her. "I was at the police station the other day, and the police told me how your pony got there. I thought it might make a story. They said he belonged to you. Could we have a few facts and a picture?"

"He did belong to us," Emma said bitterly. "Come round to the paddock and I'll show him to you."

Her mother was busy and her father was on the telephone. Peter had gone out. She had the reporter and photographer to herself. She introduced them to Freckles and told them of his heroic dash for freedom, and his true home.

"But now," she said. "It's all changed. That riding school has found out where he is, and they're coming for him."

"Surely you won't let him go back?"

"My father says he's got to." She decided not to tell them about the plan. They might put that in the paper too.

"Well, it's very sad." The one with the notebook was scribbling furiously. "Can we take a picture of both of you, for the paper? I think we've got a good story here."

"Of course," Emma said and went and stood with her arms round Freckles' neck. Freckles kept butting her with his head, and then bit her finger.

"Please smile," said the photographer.

Emma did her best.

The next day, when she had finished breakfast, Emma announced that she was going for a long ride.

"I'll see you off," said her mother, "and make sure you've pulled the girths tight."

"There's no need to, really," Emma replied. "You needn't keep reminding me, you know."

Her mother insisted, so Emma was unable to take any provisions with her. She had to set off towards the Common instead of going the way she meant to take.

"Mothers can be a nuisance," she muttered to Freckles as she trotted along.

When she was sure her mother was no longer watching she turned back and took a track along the side of the golf course. Freckles loved this gallop. The difficulty was making him stop before the track ended in a path which crossed the course. It was a public right of way but not a bridle path, as she had been forcibly told many times by the groundsman and enraged golfers. Once again he insisted on continuing along the path.

"Freckles! No!" she cried. "We're going a different way today. We don't want to be seen."

With a tremendous effort she managed to turn him and stop him without falling off. They were in the middle of a little oak wood and Freckles started to eat the acorns which lay on the ground.

"It's all very well for you," she cried, in an outburst of tearful rage. "You don't know how important it is to get you hidden today. It's lucky I managed to stop you. I think I'd better lead you out now."

She dismounted and led him back along the path, then turned left towards the scrubby heathland which bordered the course. Once away from the golf course and hidden from it by a line of trees she remounted and made her way across sandy humps and hillocks in the general direction of what she hoped was the railway.

"It might be easier by the road, Freckles," she told him, "but today we want to keep away from people."

She tried to visualise the way she had come before, by bicycle, to work out where Esmé's allotment must be.

"Perhaps I'm just going round in circles," she told herself dejectedly, "because I can't see it anywhere."

Then suddenly she stumbled across the track which ran by the railway, and the track took her to the allotment, where Esmé, Joanna and Kathy were waiting for her.

"We thought you were never coming," Joanna told her.

"We were just about to go home."

"I'm glad you didn't. I got lost," Emma explained. "I'm really stiff."

"I'll take off his saddle and bridle and rub him down," cried Kathy. "I know how to do it."

Emma sank down on one of the upturned boxes outside the shed. As she watched Freckles grazing contentedly on the overgrown cabbages and lettuces, she recounted her interview with the young reporter.

"I'll take four copies of the paper from our shop," Kathy cried. "Then we needn't pay for them."

"It won't do that Captain Wetherby any good when people read how he's behaved," Joanna said. "They'll boo him in the streets, I shouldn't wonder. What do you think he'll do when he comes tomorrow and finds out Freckles is missing?"

"He won't be able to do anything. He'll just have to go home again." Emma sounded more confident than she felt.

"He sounds the sort of man who won't just do that," warned Esmé. "Do you think we'll have to keep Freckles here for ever? If we do, whatever are we going to feed him on? He's eaten quite a lot already."

"That's why I told you to bring provisions. We must have food here for him, and for us. One of us has to be here to guard him all the time during the day, and put him in the shed if anyone comes along. Joe's made a lot of hay. I'm really tired but I think we should cycle home and fetch as much as we can. Who'll stay to guard Freckles?"

"I will," Kathy volunteered. "You haven't got a bike here but you can borrow mine."

"Much good biscuits will do, and nuts." Esmé was scornful as the three rode along, leaving Kathy behind.

"Well, it will all help. I meant pony nuts, of course, not ordinary nuts."

"How do you expect me to get pony nuts?"

"Carrots! You can get carrots, or swedes, or

125

mangelwurzels. They'll keep him going. Let's all of us bring as many carrots as we can tomorrow. And we've got some pony nuts in the garage at home, if I can get them out without anyone seeing. Luckily the hay is stored in his shed in the paddock, where Mum can't see. Let's go there first and load up. I know where to find some sacks."

"I don't know what's going to happen next, really I don't," Esmé grumbled as they trudged back to Freckles, their bicycle baskets full of pony nuts and the sacks of hay loaded on to their saddles. "I don't know why we're doing all this for you."

"I don't know either," Joanna backed her up.

"Oh, please, Esmé. We can't let him go back to that place. You know what a state he was in."

"Yes, but what's going to happen?" Esmé asked.

Emma was soon to find out.

The next day, before they had even finished breakfast, Captain Wetherby arrived with his horse box at the yard gate.

Emma's father, forgetting that Nelson was sitting on his shoulder, opened the back door. Nelson, who had a passion for shoes, fluttered down and immediately grabbed one of Captain Wetherby's.

"Get that bird off," the Captain shrieked, waving his foot about. Nelson clung on even harder.

"Keep still," cried Alison. "It makes him worse if you move. Peter, get your father's walking stick. Nelson will climb on to that."

"That parrot needs to be knocked senseless, that's what it needs," roared Captain Wetherby.

"If you don't watch out, you'll be knocked senseless," muttered Emma.

By this time Nelson had actually bitten through the shoe.

"I'll sue you, he's ruined my shoe and he's got my toe." Captain Wetherby was hysterical.

"This may call for surgery," said Emma's father, who had managed to persuade Nelson to move on to the walking stick and return to his aviary.

"Go and fetch Freckles, Emma," said Alison. "We'd better give Captain Wetherby some coffee."

"I don't need any coffee," he shouted. "I just want to get out of this madhouse!"

Emma came back from the paddock.

"Freckles isn't there," she announced.

"Not there! Where is he?"

"He's not there."

Captain Wetherby was apoplectic with rage. Stretched out in a chair, very red in the face, with his shoe and sock off and a dressing on one toe, he waved his foot up and down and shouted at Emma. "You get that pony, and be quick about it. I'm not going back without him."

"Emma! Where is he?" By this time her father was shouting too. "If he's in my vegetable garden …" He rushed out of the back door, summoning Peter to follow him.

Alison turned to Emma. "Where is Freckles?" she asked, very quietly.

"He's not in his paddock, or his stable. I told you."

"And is that all you're going to say?"

"Yes."

"She needs horsewhipping, that's what she needs." Captain Wetherby was pulling on his sock and shoe. "What's she done with him?"

He rose and walked towards Emma, picking up the stick on the way. She shrank back.

"Captain Wetherby." Alison put herself between them. "I must ask you to leave now. At once. Before you do something for which you'll be sorry. We'll see you get the pony back."

Emma had never seen her mother like this, icily calm but dangerous.

Captain Wetherby was the first to look away.

"Well, just see you do," he said. "I'm not giving up. I'll take you to court."

With that he hobbled out of the door, just as the others returned. They could hear him shouting as he drove away.

"Looked everywhere for that pony," Peter said. "He seems to have vanished off the face of the earth."

"I had to get that man out," said Alison. "He was getting dangerous. He says he'll take us to court."

"And it's not an idle threat. He'll ask for heavy damages," Emma's father groaned as he sank down into a chair and put his head in his hands. "We must find that pony."

Alison went thoughtfully to the stove, looking over her shoulder at Emma as she went. There was an ominous silence.

Avoiding her mother's eye, Emma sidled out of the door.

Half an hour later, when her father had left the house, she came in again and told her mother that she was going to look for Freckles. Alison, still in the same strange, quiet mood, looked at her long and searchingly, before continuing to clear the breakfast table.

"Do you want to tell me anything else?" she asked.

Emma hung her head, but did not reply. She was certain of one thing: nothing on earth was going to make her tell them where Freckles was hidden.

She got out her bicycle and went off to visit him.

Chapter Eighteen

"This can't go on much longer," Esmé said gloomily.

It was three days later, and she and Emma and Joanna were mucking out the shed where Freckles spent his nights, locked in for safety.

"I've never seen such a mess, and we've no more straw to spread for him."

"Not much more hay either." Emma was equally gloomy.

They looked out at Freckles, who had made a desert of the allotment and was now craning his neck over the wire to try to get at some cow parsley growing on the embankment.

"He needs fresh grass badly. Perhaps we could take it in turns to lead him around outside a bit."

"Well, I can't spare the time," Joanna said firmly. "I'm already so tired doing a paper round morning and evening to get the money to buy carrots for him that I can hardly bicycle out here to take my watch."

"And I've borrowed the money from the teapot on the mantelpiece," Esmé complained. "Mum's sure to find out soon. Then there'll be big trouble. And she keeps asking me where I'm going all the time. I'm sure she's putting two and two together. She seems to spend a lot of time with your mother at the Citizens Advice Bureau."

"My mother spends more time there than she does at home," Emma told them. "She and Dad were having a row about it the other day. He told her that I was out of control because she wasn't at home enough. They've started discussing boarding school, but if they think I'm going to one of those places they can just think again. And they keep asking me where Freckles is. I tell you, it's no fun at home at the moment."

"I wonder where Kathy is. It's not like her to be late. It's her watch soon." Esmé heaved out a great forkful of sodden straw on to the heap outside and went to look over the fence.

Kathy appeared on her bicycle, waving a newspaper.

"It's here," she cried, "the article. I could only get one copy, because Dad was watching. There's a photograph of you and Freckles on the front page."

Emma snatched the paper from her and they all crowded round to look.

"You look pretty awful, Emma," Esmé said, peering over her shoulder. "But Freckles looks really handsome."

"It makes him out to be a real hero," cried Joanna, taking the paper. "There's more over the page. There's even a poem about him."

"Oh, read it out, Joanna. You're good at poetry. Let's go over and you recite it to him."

"Freckles, this is your poem," Emma said solemnly as Joanna read what the reporter had written.

"It's a lovely poem," Esmé said when Joanna had finished. "It rhymes and everything. Did you know the reporter was going to write it?"

"Of course I didn't. He never said anything about writing a poem. But he did seem upset that Freckles might have to go back. Perhaps that's why he did it. So people wouldn't want him to have to return to the riding school."

"That's all very well." Esmé was stubbing the ground with her foot. "It doesn't solve the problem of what to do now. How can we go on hiding him with no food, and no money to buy any more? What are we going to do?"

"How much money have we all got?" Emma asked, after a pause.

"I've three pounds left from my paper round," Joanna told her.

"And I've two pounds from helping in the shop evenings," said Kathy.

"And I spent all the teapot money on carrots, and there they are." Esmé pointed to two large carrier bags sitting on the ground outside the shed.

"The only thing to do then," Emma went on, "is for you all to give me the money you've got, and I'll add it to mine, and I'll go along and buy a rope and one of those head collars with a swivel on it, the sort the gypsies use. Joe told me that unless you have one of those for tethering horses they get completely tangled up. Then tomorrow I'll put him out to graze the waste ground round here, and take the first watch. Then if we all keep our watch, and only put him in at night, and get mangelwurzels from the edge of a field I know of, we ought to be able to keep going for a bit longer."

"But how much longer?"

"Oh, Esmé, I don't know. Captain Wetherby's asking some judge to say he can have Freckles back, but the judge might not agree, I don't know. We must just hope."

"We'd better shut him in now with what's left of the hay and some carrots because the time's getting on and I must get home – unless any of you want to stay on with him."

"Give me your money first then," Emma said, "and I'll

go shopping tomorrow morning early. Then we'll all meet here as usual."

"How much longer?" groaned Esmé as she wheeled her bicycle under the wire. "I'm sure Mum's getting on to us and when Dad sees his so-called allotment there'll be big trouble."

"It's exciting, though," said Joanna.

"We might end up getting our pictures in the paper, too!" Kathy had been greatly impressed by the article.

Emma led Freckles into the shed and locked him in. Things were desperate, but at least no one had found him yet.

"Emma, why didn't you call me to talk to that reporter?" her mother asked when she got home.

"You were busy, and I only told him the truth."

"You look pretty weird in the photograph," Peter told her.

"Oh, shut up."

"There's the telephone again," said her mother. "It'll be someone else ringing up to ask about Freckles, and I don't know where he is. It's all very worrying."

"Seen this article?" asked Emma's father, banging down the paper he had brought in. "More unwelcome publicity. I wish, Emma, that you'd think before you give interviews. This may prejudice the case. Captain Wetherby may say that we're trying to influence the court. We ought to know by tomorrow whether he's obtained his order or not."

"How did the hearing go?" Alison asked.

"Peter's friend Steve gave evidence of what went on at the riding school. I think the judge was impressed. The poor boy's unemployed now, he tells me. Then the veterinary report helped too. But we can't get over the fact that Freckles belongs there now, and not to us. I've always told you that," he said, turning to Emma. "For the last time, Emma, I'm asking you: where is that pony?"

"And for the last time I'm telling you, I can't tell you."

Early the next morning Emma set out for the saddler's shop. She had just enough money to buy a collar with a swivel and a short piece of rope. Then she went off to the allotment.

"I'm really tired with all this cycling," she told the others. "I'll go and find a good place to tie him up, with plenty of grass, and then come back. Any of you brought anything to eat?"

"I've got some sweets," said Kathy, "and four tins of Seven-Up."

"You're lucky having a shop," Emma told her. "I wish we had one. I've just brought some of my breakfast."

"I've brought some apples." Joanna held up a paper bag.

"And I've managed a packet of biscuits," Esmé said. "Couldn't get hold of anything else."

"We'll have a feast, then, when I get back."

Emma led Freckles away and the others settled down on the ground to wait.

"He seems really happy," she told them when she came back. "He's got plenty to eat now. No need to worry about him, but I'll keep going to have a look just in case."

When they had eaten everything they had brought, the four lay back and let the sun beat down on them.

"This is perfect," said Esmé, taking off her T-shirt. "A really hot August day for once, with not a cloud in the sky, and no one anywhere around."

"My father's playing in a golf match," Emma told them. "I hope he wins. Then he'll be in a good temper for the rest of the day."

Soon they were all sound asleep.

Much later, when she awoke, Emma remembered Freckles. "I'd better move him to fresh ground," she said. "Wait here for me."

Within minutes she came running back.

"He's gone!" she cried. "He's pulled the rope away, and I can't see him anywhere."

"That animal!" groaned Esmé as she got unwillingly to her feet. Joanna and Kathy, rubbing their eyes, scrambled up too.

"I suppose we'll all have to look for him," Esmé went on. "We'll go different ways and meet back here in half an hour. I'll have to be getting off then. Do you know how late it is?"

"Better take some carrots." Emma gave them all a handful. "And here are a few of the last of the pony nuts. You won't catch him without."

Each one had the same story to tell when they met up again.

"He just seems to have vanished into thin air," groaned Emma. "What are we to do now?"

"We'll have to go home. I'm getting really hungry," Esmé said. "You ring us if you have any news."

"I'm hungry too," said Joanna.

"And me," said Kathy.

"We'd better go then." Emma was nearly in tears. "Perhaps he'll come back here. I'll leave the wire open for him and some carrots in the shed."

Very despondently, she set off for home.

Chapter Nineteen

Emma nearly fainted with surprise as she wheeled her bicycle in through the gate, for there in the yard stood Freckles, munching hay.

"How in the world did you get here?" she gasped. "Oh, I am glad to see you. I'd better take you round to the paddock or you'll be in the garden next."

Emma gathered up the remains of the hay and led Freckles through the gate.

He nuzzled her neck as she settled him with more hay and filled his water trough. Then she went back into the yard and through the kitchen door.

Her mother and father were sitting at the table. Peter had not come in yet and she was greeted with stony silence. Only Nelson croaked a welcome. She went over to his aviary and stroked the top of his head, feeling her face getting redder and redder.

"I see he's back," she said at last. "Where did you find him?"

"Your father lost his match," said her mother.

"How? Why?"

"He found Freckles on the golf course. He had to break off in the middle to telephone me to fetch him."

"I'm sorry about that."

"And you know all about it, don't you?" roared her father. "You tethered him somewhere near there in the first place, didn't you?"

"Yes, but I didn't mean him to stray on to the golf course."

"You never mean anything, do you? You never foresee the consequences of anything you do." Her father was still shouting. "But the result was that pony ruined my match, and spoiled several greens on the course. As captain this

year, what am I supposed to do about that? Stop your pocket money again, I suppose. A lot of good that will do! And why was he grazing where he was? Just speak the truth for once."

"It's no good pretending any more, Emma," her mother put in. "I know where you've been hiding him. Esmé's mother and I worked it out and went to look this afternoon. You realise, Esmé will get into a lot of trouble over this, don't you?"

Emma hung her head and her eyes filled with tears.

"I didn't want him to go back," she said. "That's why I hid him, and Esmé and Joanna and Kathy helped me. I don't want any of them to get into trouble. I just want to be able to keep Freckles, that's all."

"I'm sorry, Emma, but you must learn that you can't always get your own way. The order was made by the court today. We have one week in which to return Freckles to the riding school."

"Oh, but that's not possible! You saw how he'd been treated. We can't send him back there."

"We can and we must, so just sit down and eat your tea." Her father returned to his paper.

"Sausages, chips, baked beans and fried egg, Emma," her mother said from the stove. "I'm sure you're ready for it. Why, what's the matter?"

Emma had sunk down into the armchair where Solomon usually sat and gone very white. Her head seemed to be going round and round, and everything in the kitchen was getting more and more blurred. "So it was all no good," she murmured and closed her eyes.

When she opened them again her mother and father were both bending over her.

"Here, drink this, Emma," said her father. "It will make you feel better."

"You should try to eat," said her mother as she put a tray on her lap. "I don't suppose you've had anything much all

139

day. And things aren't as bad as your father made out."

"What do you mean?" Emma asked faintly.

"Well, it seems that the Council are to inspect the riding school. Its licence comes up for renewal this week. After what's come out about it they may not renew it."

"Then what will happen?"

"If Captain Wetherby's licence is taken away he can't run a riding school. So Freckles may not have to go back. Now, please be sensible and have your tea."

"I don't know if I can believe you," Emma said slowly.

She looked at her father's face. It was still set and stern. Without saying anything he got up and went out of the room, and she heard him pick up the telephone.

"He wants him to go back," she cried. "He doesn't want him here. He's telephoning Captain Wetherby to come and get him. Oh, Mum, what shall I do?"

"He's not telephoning Captain Wetherby. Don't be silly, Emma. There's plenty of time yet for things to change. You must be patient."

"How can I be patient with this hanging over me? I must go and see Freckles now and make some plans."

"You're not to make any more plans," her mother called as she went out of the door, but Emma had already gone, taking a handful of carrots with her as she went.

In the paddock, as she fed Freckles the carrots, she made her next plan. Whatever her mother said, she was sure her father was talking to Captain Wetherby, and that arrangements were being made for him to come and fetch Freckles. She couldn't take him back to the allotment, and she couldn't get her friends into any more trouble by asking them to help her. The only thing she could do was to run away with him again, before Captain Wetherby came.

Once she had made her decision, Emma felt much happier. She settled Freckles for the night and went back into the house.

Peter was alone in the kitchen and Emma told him about Freckles' return and Captain Wetherby's order. "But he's not getting Freckles back," she went on. "I've got another plan."

"Oh, no! You and your plans. Well, don't tell me, then I can't give it away to anyone. Do you know that Captain Wetherby forced Steve to tell him our address, really forced him? But don't do anything silly. We need you here because" – he looked round and his voice sank to a whisper – "those hens are being freed at dawn tomorrow by the Animal Rights Brigade. They've made their arrangements."

"That's good," said Emma. "That should teach Mr Giles a lesson. I promise I'll be here to see what happens. After that – who knows."

Chapter Twenty

The house was quiet, bathed in moonlight. Emma was dreaming that she was a turtle, swimming through a creamy sea. Then suddenly she felt a hand on her shoulder, tugging her awake. Peter was leaning over her.

"We've done it!" he said. "They've been freed. Be seeing you." And stole out of her room again.

Emma tossed in her bed. What was going to happen now? What would Mr Giles do when he found out? How would he behave? Who would he blame? Then she was fast asleep again.

She awoke to the banging of doors, and bright lights outside her window, which faced the road. There were two police cars out there.

They'd come for him. They'd come for Peter. She was sure of it. Poor Peter! And he'd really done it for her sake. She imagined him in jail, eating bread and water. His friends too – all in separate cells. And the animals locked up again. And Mr Giles gloating over them. Mr Giles, with his horrible ginger hair and red face.

She got out of bed and went across the corridor to Peter's room. She opened the door and peered in. He was fast asleep in bed, his hand thrown across his face.

"It's not that, then," she thought. "What is it?"

She went back to her room and looked out of the window again. Then she put on her dressing gown and slippers and went downstairs and sat by herself in the kitchen. She could hear voices in the hall. Her mother came in, also in her dressing gown.

"What's the matter, Mum?" Emma asked.

"There's been a burglary. All Mr Giles' hens have gone. I've told the police we don't know anything about it. We don't, do we?"

"I've made some tea. Here's a cup for you. You must need it."

"Why this sudden solicitude?" asked her mother suspiciously. "I'd better take some out to the police officers as well. They want to get back to Mr Giles' farm."

Emma sat on in the kitchen, feeding Bodger and Nelson alternately with bits of toast, and pondering.

"I wonder where they've taken those hens," she said to Peter when he came down. "I hope they have happier lives in future, wherever it is. One good thing is that Mum doesn't seem to suspect anything."

"I bet we haven't heard the last of it yet," Peter said gloomily.

Later that morning, whilst Emma was grooming Freckles in the yard and her father was out in the garden, the front doorbell rang.

"Who can that be?" Her mother, who was preparing lunch, called through the kitchen window.

"I'm busy. You answer it," called back Emma.

Her mother sighed, rinsed the flour off her hands and went out.

"I'd better wash your mane and tail too," Emma told Freckles. "If you're going to join a circus you'd better look smart. Why won't your mane lie down properly? It stands straight up, whatever I try to do to it."

She tied him to a drainpipe and went to fetch a bowl of soapy water. She was just on her way to the kitchen when her father called her into the garden, where he and her mother were standing talking to a tall, thin man wearing a tweed suit. Emma remembered him as the man who had caught Freckles and helped her when she had fallen off during that first ride on the Common.

"This is Lord Osberton, Emma," said her father. "He's come to see if he can find out anything about what happened to those hens last night. You know he owns Mr Giles' farm?"

Emma nodded.

"We've met before," said Lord Osberton. "How's your pony now? How's the training going?"

"I'm having a lot of trouble," Emma told him. "Not with the training, but with other things."

"It's a long story," said her mother. "You don't want to bother Lord Osberton with it. We're just going to have a drink and then talk to Peter."

"I'd like to hear Emma's story," said Lord Osberton. "She can show me the garden and then we'll have our drink."

He and Emma walked off. She decided to show him the ducks first, and then Freckles.

"You've certainly got a lot," he commented, surveying the fifteen ducks. Tabitha was now dwarfed by seven large drakes, and the ducks were as large as she was. "Whatever are you going to do with them all? That pond looks a bit small for them."

"It is," Emma told him, "so they keep getting out or flying over the wire into Dad's garden. He gets really angry."

"I'm not surprised. Why don't you sell a few?"

"Because then they'd get eaten at Christmas, and I don't want that. I'd like to find somewhere they could go and live happily. I'd just keep one duck, then, as a friend for Tabitha. That's Tabitha, their mother, over there, with a swing-wing." She pointed. "I helped her get a family, but they're too much for her now."

"So you want all animals to be happy, do you?"

"I do," Emma said earnestly.

Lord Osberton thought for a moment.

"Well, I've got a lake," he said at last. "Do you think they'd be happy there?"

"That's just what they want. They need more room. Because they'll start families too, quite soon, I expect."

"I'm rather afraid of that. We lost a lot of ducks, though, to foxes last year, so we could do with a few more."

"I wouldn't want them to be eaten by foxes."

"Better than being Christmas dinners. Anyway, we've built an island out in the lake now, so if they're sensible and go there at night they'll be safe."

"Can I come and see them?"

"Of course. In fact, aren't you coming to Miss Bradshaw's Pony Club Camp? It's being held on my land. You'll see the lake then."

Emma's face clouded.

"I was coming. I promised my mother I'd go – though I think most of them are terrible snobs – only I don't think I'll be here now."

"Why not?"

"Oh, I don't know. Come and see Freckles."

Emma took Lord Osberton by the hand and together they went into the yard.

"Looks a fine little pony," he said. "He should do well in the gymkhana. I'll look forward to giving you a rosette."

"The trouble is ... Haven't you heard anything, about Captain Wetherby, or Freckles?"

"I've been abroad. Just got back. The police telephoned me about Mr Giles' hens and asked me to look in."

"Well, the trouble is ... You may not believe this, but Freckles doesn't belong to us now."

"Who does he belong to?"

"This riding school, owned by Captain Wetherby. My parents sent him back to Mr Riley, the man they bought him from, when I had an accident, and Mr Riley died, so Freckles was bought by Captain Wetherby. He had such a terrible time there that he escaped and came home to us, but now the judge says he's got to go back to the riding school. And I'm not going to let him go."

"Can't you buy him back from the riding school?"

"Captain Wetherby won't sell him. He says Freckles is a useful size for him, and he's coming to get him. Do you think you could help me to keep him? I'll show you what the reporter wrote about him."

Emma pulled a copy of the newspaper article and poem out of her pocket. "I always carry this with me," she told him. "Don't you think it's a fabulous poem?"

"Very moving, certainly. I wish I could help, but I'm Chairman of the Bench and I have to uphold the law. That's why I'm investigating this matter of the hens. If the ruling is that he must go back I'm afraid he'll have to go. By the way, how was Mr Giles keeping those hens?"

"Oh, it was terrible, really cruel. He had them all in little cages, one on top of the other. They couldn't move, or scratch, or sit down properly. I'm glad they were rescued."

"You told me you wanted all animals to be happy. Did you have anything to do with it?"

Emma looked up into his face. "Do you agree with what Mr Giles did?" she asked.

"No, I don't agree with factory farming, and I don't want it on my farms. But did you have anything to do with freeing the hens? You know where they were found, don't you?"

"No. Where?"

"All over the Common."

"I certainly didn't expect that."

"You did know something was going on then, didn't you?"

"Well, I did tell Peter, and he told some friends of his at school who don't agree that animals should be treated cruelly."

"Nor do I, but the law is the law. People's rights of property must be respected. I think I'd better go and talk to Peter now. I'm sure my drink's waiting for me. I hope I see you at the Pony Club Camp, and I'll speak to your mother about the ducks."

Lord Osberton walked off and Emma fetched a bowl of water from the kitchen and started on Freckles' tail.

"It's no good," she told him. "He's a nice man, but he won't help. There's nothing for it but to run away again." She was in tears. Freckles rubbed his head against her shoulder.

Her mother and father and Lord Osberton were sitting on garden chairs on the lawn with a tray of drinks.

"Do you want anything, Emma?" her mother called.

"No thanks. I'm just going upstairs."

"Call Peter then, would you? He's doing his homework. Will you tell him we want him in the garden?"

"It's about the hens," she told him, opening his bedroom door. "There's a Lord Osberton here, and he wants to interview you."

"Oh, lor," said Peter, getting up. "If I go to jail, come and visit me with a food parcel, won't you?"

"Of course you won't go to jail. He's a kind man, but keen on law. He doesn't agree with factory farming either."

Emma went into her room and started packing as much as she could into her rucksack.

"Here we go again," she said to Freckles as she saddled

148

and bridled him in the yard and stuffed carrots into her pocket. "I hope we have better luck this time."

At the last moment she left a note for her mother on the kitchen table.

"Goodbye!" she called.

"Have a nice ride," replied her mother.

Chapter Twenty-One

It was fine at first, trotting through the early autumn countryside. The leaves were just turning colour but very few had dropped off the trees yet. Emma loved this time of year, when it was still warm, and the earth seemed to stand still, in a last glow of summer. She passed an avenue of horse chestnut trees and was tempted to stop and look for conkers, but decided to press on. As always, she talked to Freckles as she rode along.

"They may come looking for us," she told him. "It may not be long before Mum finds my note. Better not go any of the usual ways. I'll try this lane. It may lead somewhere new."

Freckles, for once, was behaving well. "I suppose he'd glad to be out," Emma thought, "after being cooped up in that allotment for so long. It would be dreadful for him to be shut up in a riding school again, and be pulled about and not given enough to eat. How could that judge order him to go back, even for a day? He can't know anything about ponies."

Soon she was in a part of the country she didn't recognise. It was flat and treeless and there were dykes between the fields, and just the occasional house or farm, where lights were beginning to appear in the windows.

She began to feel frightened. Alone under a wide sky, which glowed with a strange light as the sun started to go down, with an endless white road stretching ahead, she thought of her home, and the kitchen, so warm and comfortable, and her mother's cheerful face – cheerful, that is, until she read her note. How would her mother feel then?

It was getting colder now. In about an hour it would be dark. What would she do then, if she couldn't find anywhere to sleep? And what would her parents do, if they didn't find her? Anyway, how could they find her, in this lonely place? She remembered her mother's anguished face looking down at her after she'd run away before and Peter had brought her home. Her mother would be sure to think there would be another accident – worse perhaps this time.

That was why they had sent Freckles back to Mr Riley: they didn't want her to have another accident with him. And now here she was, running away again. It's all because of that wretched pony, her father would tell her mother. She's out of control. She ought to go to boarding school. She hasn't behaved sensibly since we first bought Freckles. That's what he would say, and perhaps he would be right. She had caused them a lot of worry, and she'd lied and been deceitful. Perhaps she ought to trust her parents more. Even if Freckles had to go back for a short time, he would return to her in the end.

She looked round at the twilit countryside, pulled Freckles up and began to cry. She let the reins hang loose and he lowered his head and began to eat the grass on the verge of the road. What should she do? Could she go home now? Peter would laugh at her, and her parents would be upset and angry. She looked up at the sky. It was getting darker all the time, and there seemed to be rain clouds on the horizon. She could not face the thought of being soaked as well as lost and made up her mind. She would go home and face the consequences, assuming she could find the way. She pulled Freckles' head up and turned him. He looked round at her.

"We're going back home, Freckles," she told him and pressed her heels into his sides. He needed no further urging. From a trot he broke into a canter and, later, into a gallop, but he was not running away with her: he was heading for home. All she had to do was to hold on. She trusted him absolutely. It was like that first ride at Mr Riley's.

"Oh, Freckles," she sobbed as she hung on to his mane, "I love you so much."

He pricked up his ears and went faster.

They arrived at the yard gate as darkness fell. Peter heard the clatter of hooves and went out to meet them. He helped to take off Freckles' bridle and saddle and rubbed him down. Then together they spread straw in the stable and gave Freckles a hay net. Only then did he turn to Emma. "You nearly frightened them to death, you know, with your note," he said. "They're out looking for you now. I'm not going to support you any more if you do things like that. They're only doing their best. Why don't you start to grow up a bit?"

"I know." Emma was sobbing again. "I will try. I just get so upset when I think I can't keep Freckles. But I love Mum and Dad too. I don't want to hurt them."

"Anyway, you needn't have worried. After you'd gone, and luckily before we went into the kitchen and found your note, Steve came round and told us that the Council had inspected the riding school and that they're going to oppose the renewal of Captain Wetherby's licence. It comes up in court next week. In the meantime Dad says Freckles can stay here. It's lucky he can't stand that Captain Wetherby. So there! You see! You needn't have worried. Justice always triumphs in the end," he finished, a little pompously.

"Oh, does it? What about the hens? I suppose they've all been shut up again."

"No, they haven't. Lord Osberton went round to see Mr Giles and had a row with him. Told him he wouldn't allow any intensive methods on his farms. Dad went with him and told us about it afterwards."

"What happened to the hens?"

"All of us who had had anything to do with it had to help collect them from the Common and take them back to Mr Giles. It was a terrible job, I can tell you. Took us all afternoon. He's had to promise to keep them on free range in future. They're in that big field at the back of his farmhouse, where they used to be. A lot of them were in a really bad way: they'd lost most of their feathers and could hardly stand."

"It's lucky I went and looked when I did or they'd have been in a worse state. I don't think those sheds have been there very long."

"Then we had to fix up perches and laying boxes in the barn. When we'd finished Lord Osberton said he'd forget the matter and called off the police."

"So, that's all right, then. I'm starving. I suppose there's no supper left?"

"Here they are. You'd better find out.'

The car drew up and Emma tumbled into her mother's arms. "I'll never frighten you again," she cried. "I'll never run away again."

"I should hope not," said her father. "We can't take much more. You must talk to us in future before you take matters into your own hands."

"I'll try to."

"And not deceive us again?" asked her mother.

"I'll try not to."

"Come in and have some supper then."

Emma stroked Bodger and Solomon, both asleep by the stove, and settled down at the kitchen table. She looked round contentedly. "Oh, I love being home," she said. "Don't ever send me away from home."

"It's you who seems to spend your whole time trying to leave it," Peter told her as he cut himself a slice of bread and cheese.

At the weekend Steve visited Peter.

"Captain Wetherby's done a bunk," he told him. "Gone off with whatever money he could lay his hands on and gone to live in Spain. He'd got so unpopular, I'm not surprised."

"What's happening to the horses?" Emma asked.

"They're to be sold. The British Horse Society's dealing with it. They've asked me to look after things for the moment. Then I'll be out of a job again, I expect. They're going to try to make sure all the ponies go to good homes."

"Freckles has a good home here, hasn't he, Dad?" Emma put her arm through her father's. He had come up from the garden and had been listening. "You can buy him back now. He's not going anywhere else ever, is he?"

"You seem to have won in the end," he answered. "But just make sure you keep him out of my garden, and get rid of those ducks."

"It's lucky I entered you for the Pony Club Camp," said her mother. "We could bring them when we come to the jumping on the last day, since Lord Osberton has agreed to let the ducks go on his lake."

"You don't mean I've got to go to the Pony Club Camp with all those snobs?" cried Emma.

"Now Emma. You promised. Remember!"

"Oh, well," she conceded. "I suppose I'll have to go. I might take the Institute of the Horse exams. That would show Doreen."

"First I should learn not to fall off so often, if I were you," advised Peter.

"Don't discourage her, Peter," Alison told him. "She could be a good rider if she tried. And you have promised to try, haven't you, Emma?"

Chapter
Twenty-Two

"**W**hy do I have to go? Freckles is behaving perfectly. And it's the last week of the holidays. What a waste!"

"You're booked in, and you're going. What about all your good resolutions? I should get on with some training if I were you, and Freckles looks as if he needs brushing. You want to do well, don't you? You owe it to Miss Bradshaw, after what happened last time." Her mother went back into the house and shut the door.

Kathy, called on to help, was only too willing to brush, and oil hooves, help clean the tack, and replace the jumps when Freckles knocked them down.

"Glad you don't need me so much now," said Joe, coming up to watch. "If you can keep that pony's back legs up and manage not to fall off he should do well at jumping."

"That's what I'm hoping. Mum rang up, and it seems it will be mostly jumping, and dressage, and cross-country, and treasure hunts. I'm going to concentrate on jumping. The one who does best in everything gets a cup."

"What's dressage?" asked Kathy.

"I think you just have to walk up to lines and stand on them. As Freckles won't keep still I don't think we'll be much good at that. Anyway, it sounds boring."

"I wish I had a pony," sighed Kathy. "Will you give me a ride now?"

Emma led her round the paddock, trying to instruct her on how to rise to the trot.

"It makes me feel seasick," Kathy told her.

"And it gets me out of breath," said Emma.

Riding along to the Camp, early on a fine September

morning, with her belongings in a rucksack strapped across the saddle, Emma dreamed again of glory: Anne, pushed into second or third place, or no place at all, looked on enviously as Emma received yet another red rosette. "You've got a really promising young rider there," she imagined Lord Osberton telling Miss Bradshaw. "What a combination they make. The girl is a natural horsewoman." "There have been times ..." Miss Bradshaw would reply, but she would be cut short by Lord Osberton. "Did you see how she took that jump? Perfect timing, and no pull on his mouth." "At first I thought he was too strong for her," Doreen would be saying. "Now I think they might be ready for the White City. The only difficulty is finding other competitors of her standard ..."

Two hours later she was trotting through Osberton Hall's wide entrance gates, past the two lodges on either side, with smoke curling from their chimneys, and down the drive to the stable block where the Camp was to be housed.

Miss Bradshaw greeted her coldly. Emma saw she was still walking with a stick. Doreen assigned Freckles to his stable, and Emma to her bunk.

"Breakfast at nine-thirty," she said. "Then all out for inspection."

Miss Bradshaw sat in the middle of the circle on her shooting stick.

"I wonder she dares do that, with you know who present," Anne remarked to her companion in Emma's hearing. Emma ignored her.

"Amanda, your stirrups are too long. Betsy, your bridle's a disgrace. David, don't hold your reins so tight. Peggy, your girth's slipping," Miss Bradshaw would call, and the line would halt until matters had been righted. Doreen rearranged the line of ponies, with the smallest at the back. Freckles was placed behind Starlight. Miss Bradshaw gave the order to canter.

Anne had let her hair grow. It now hung in a pigtail below her hat, tied at the bottom with a green bow.

"You must not, Freckles! Stop, Freckles!" Emma was whispering furiously as Freckles, intrigued by the bow, edged closer to Starlight. Anne looked round and glared at Emma. Freckles suddenly broke ranks and came up alongside Starlight. He tried to grab the bow but instead rubbed his nose along Anne's gleaming cream jacket and jodhpurs, leaving long green streaks.

"Stop it!" cried Anne. "Look what he's doing." She lashed out with her crop, but Freckles drew back.

"Whatever's happening there?" called Miss Bradshaw.

"Somehow I thought it would be you," she said when Freckles and Emma had been summoned into the centre of the ring. "You can't control your pony, can you, Emma?"

"Yes, I can. I just wasn't thinking. I was thinking about something else. If I'd known what he was doing I'd have stopped him."

"Well, pay attention then. I'm putting you behind Domino now. If Freckles gets too near he'll kick. And you'd better apologise to Anne."

"You knew perfectly well what was happening," Anne said later. "You've ruined my clothes, and we get points for a good turnout. You're a menace, that's what you are."

"Take no notice," David told Emma. His pony Trigger had also been in trouble. "You haven't been to one of these camps before, have you? I'll show you round if you like."

"Would you walk round the Cross-country with me? I'm terrified I won't manage that."

"I never knew Lord Osberton had such a huge estate," Emma said, as they were trudging round. "Hills, and valleys and – oh, there's the lake – that's where the ducks are going to be."

The lake was shaded by sycamores and willows. Beyond it stood a great house with a pillared doorway and stone steps leading up to it, flanked on either side by urns. Swans and cygnets were sailing on the water, and mallards dabbling round the banks.

"I'd love to live here," sighed Emma. "What a marvellous place for animals. It's a waste, having it all to himself. He's away travelling a lot too, Mum says."

"I've heard they want to run some road through the park."

"Hope they don't. We've enough cars littering up the place already."

"Well, do you think you'll manage it?" David asked as they turned back towards the stable block.

"Manage it! I'll be lucky if I stay on after the first jump. It looks a terrible course to me."

"Trigger nearly finished once. Came down at that jump with the gate and ditch in front. You just have to push on and hope for the best."

The next day Emma stood at the starting line with Freckles. At last her name was called.

As so often happened when she least expected it, Freckles took charge. He set off at a great speed, and then settled down, negotiating each jump carefully. All she had to do was to cling on. This is too good to be true, Emma thought: I may win the cup at this rate. Then at Jump 15, the Water Jump, Freckles decided he had had enough. He refused three times and nothing would make him go on.

Doreen was officiating at the jump.

"Just for once that pony should be made to do something he doesn't want to," she said. "Get off, Emma. I'll take him over it."

She mounted, borrowed a riding crop, and gave Freckles a good smack with it. He snorted with surprise.

"Now, up and over," she said.

Freckles went up, but he did not go over. Instead he gave one of the enormous bucks of which only he was capable and Doreen went over his head into the water. Emma shuddered. Nobody dared to laugh. Doreen sat on the bank, emptying water out of her hat and her boots, and wringing out her coat. She looked like Emma after one of her wilder rides.

But not for nothing was Doreen trying for her British Horse Society Test, Stage 4. She approached Freckles again. He was innocently nibbling at a patch of grass, with Emma holding his bridle and whispering to him to behave.

"Now, Freckles," she said. "You *are* going over that water jump."

Freckles ears' went back.

By this time word had got round about Doreen's strange appearance and practically the whole camp was assembled at the Water Jump to see what would happen next.

Emma knew Freckles loved an audience. This time he appeared to decide that he would show them what he could do if he really tried. When Doreen mounted again and set him at the jump, this time without using her crop, he flew over it like a bird. "There, you see," she said, still dripping but triumphant, as she patted him and then handed him back to Emma, "he needs firm handling, that's all. He's a good little pony, really."

Watching him look sideways at Doreen, Emma was not so sure. She felt he had not forgotten her use of the riding crop, and that there might be trouble yet.

"Doreen tells me that she thinks Freckles could be really good at jumping, providing you learn to control him properly," Miss Bradshaw told Emma at lunch that day. "I'll give you a lesson on your own after tea. Be at the gate to the smaller field at five o'clock," she said and stalked away, leaving Emma gazing after her.

Miss Bradshaw was waiting with her shooting stick as Emma rode up to the gate.

Together they replaced the jumps that had been knocked down earlier in the afternoon.

"Now, get ready, Emma," Miss Bradshaw said once the field was clear. "When I give the word, you canter smartly into the ring." She opened the gate and put a restraining arm across it.

Freckles took no notice of the restraining arm. As soon as the gate was opened he charged in. Miss Bradshaw's arm was spun round across her body and she collapsed with a gasp of pain. Doreen hurried to her assistance and led her away, gazing back reproachfully at Emma as she went. "You'd better try a few jumps on your own," she said. "I hope Miss Bradshaw isn't seriously hurt."

Parents' Day came at last. Emma had not done well in dressage, but she had picked up a good many points in her second cross-country trial, and in the treasure hunt, and her spirits were high. "If you behave, and lift your feet up, and jump properly," she told Freckles as she groomed him, "we may beat Anne. I'll be happy if we just do that."

Senior jumping was first, so Emma had a chance to look round before the junior jumping started. There were bales of straw for the competitors' parents to sit on and a table at one end set out with cups and trophies and rosettes, behind which Lord Osberton and Miss Bradshaw were installed. Miss Bradshaw had her arm in a sling. Her shooting stick was by her side. She was talking earnestly to Lord Osberton as she pointed out the competitors to him.

Emma's parents were late. She couldn't see them anywhere, until at last she caught sight of a dismal little procession straggling across from the direction of the lake, with her mother and father at the fore, followed by Joe, then Peter and Alan. They all looked very tired, and her father's hair, she noticed, was wet and his clothes were muddy.

She went over to meet them. "What happened to you?" she cried.

"Had a terrible time," said her mother shortly. "Those ducks! It took us all morning to catch them."

"Dad tried a rugby tackle," said Peter, "and went into the pond."

"I don't wish to discuss the matter," their father snorted.

"We couldn't have managed without Joe," her mother told her, "so we brought him along."

"We left one behind for you," Alan put in. "To be Tabitha's friend."

"I only hope it wasn't a drake," said Peter. "If it was we can't change them now. The others are on the lake."

"A drake!" Emma's father's voice rose to an anguished wail. "If we have any more ducklings I'm moving out. I'm taking a room in town."

"No, it weren't a drake, sir. I'm certain of that." Joe was reassuring. "It were the little swing-wing, I think." He turned to Emma. "The one you wanted."

"That's all right, then," said Emma. "Come along, and I'll find you some good seats. I'm jumping after tea."

"What's Miss Bradshaw done to her arm?" asked her mother.

Emma didn't answer and left them to try some practice jumping on Freckles.

Whether it was the tea her father bought her, or the beautiful September day, or the sight of Lord Osberton smiling at her, or the knowledge that the ducks were now safely on his lake, Emma did not know, but the fact remained that she and Freckles jumped one clear round after another, as the bars were raised ever higher.

Finally, only Freckles and Starlight were left in the jump-off. It was against the clock and Anne had been drawn to jump first.

Starlight's foot just touched one post: it wobbled but stayed on and Anne had jumped a clear round.

Then it was Freckles' turn. Emma knew she must be fast

to beat Anne's time. Freckles entered the ring at tremendous speed and took the first jump too high. She had a great deal of trouble staying on, but she managed it. Then he settled down, and Emma resolved to concentrate, hard. Remembering all that she had been taught, she took him under firm control. She paced him correctly for each jump; she used her hands and her legs to turn and guide him safely and surely from one jump to another in the shortest possible time; she moved with him so that he recovered his balance and speed after each jump and was ready for the next. She was oblivious of the spectators: it was just Freckles and herself. She felt as if she were riding in a dream, but this was not one of her day dreams: this was real riding, and Freckles was responding as she had never known he could. She beat Anne's time by a second.

Emma had never heard such cheering. She had not realised how popular Freckles had become since his story had got into the papers.

As the three winners lined up to receive their rosettes Lord Osberton congratulated her. "That was good riding." Then he turned to Miss Bradshaw. "She's got a smart pony there, don't you think?" he asked.

Miss Bradshaw, her arm in a sling, seemed about to reply, but in the end said nothing.

As Emma left the ring someone touched her arm. It was the young reporter, with his camerman, and behind him stood Esmé and Joanna and Kathy.

"We've been talking to him," said Esmé, nodding to the reporter. "He wants to take all our pictures."

"I've heard how you hid Freckles," said the reporter. "I think it was a brave thing to do."

"We got into a lot of trouble for it," Esmé told him. "I hope Emma doesn't make us do anything like that again."

"You never know with Emma," put in Joanna. "Anyway, please take our picture whilst the sun's out. This is my best dress."

"And I'm in my jeans because I want a ride," said Kathy.

They were interrupted by the sound of Emma's father calling her.

She looked round and saw that Miss Bradshaw and Doreen were talking to her parents, who were both looking very grave.

Chapter
Twenty-Three

"Well, what did the old warhorse have to say to you?"

Emma looked round. She was riding Freckles home from the Pony Club Camp, glancing down constantly at the red rosette pinned to his bridle. Esmé, Joanna and Kathy had come up on their bicycles and were wobbling round her as they tried to slow down to Freckles' walking pace.

"Oh, nothing much. All about having to be the one in control. She's not so bad, really. She did congratulate me on my jumping. I had to apologise, though, about her arm, and promise Mum and Dad I'd go for a lesson every Saturday morning. I suppose now they'll expect me to work at riding."

"That means you can't come into town, to the Arndale, then," Esmé said.

"There'd have been too much fuss about my going

anyway. You know Mum. She's like an elephant, never forgets a thing."

"I don't think I'm going round the shops any more, either," Kathy told them. "I'm going to save up to buy jodhpurs, and a riding hat, and then to have proper lessons."

Her friends turned off for home and Emma continued on her own, up the lane, and then by a roundabout route

along the field paths which she knew so well. Freckles was tired now, and content to walk. There was no need to hurry. She talked to him as they rode along.

"I had to apologise," she told him. "After all, you did shoot through that gate and sprain her arm. You must learn not to be so headstrong."

Freckles pricked up his ears and tried to quicken his pace, but she restrained him. Pleased with herself, she continued to lecture him.

"You do need more training," she went on, "and so do I, I expect. Miss Bradshaw says we've got possibilities. Just think of that, Freckles!"

For answer, he tried to grab at some overhanging leaves. After a brief tussle, they went on again, Freckles with a branch hanging from his mouth. She looked round her contentedly. An autumn mist was settling on the fields, and the sun was low in the West. It would soon be time to shut Freckles in his stable every night with his hay net. She loved the sound as he munched his hay, and the sweet smell it gave out, and Freckles' warm breath when she rubbed her nose against his. Then it would be winter, with fires, and snow perhaps, and Freckles breathing steam through his nostrils as she went to let him out of his stable on frosty mornings. They would gallop over the stubble fields, and go on expeditions through the dark leafless woods, and across the Common, where she had first met Lord Osberton.

They rejoined the road and passed by the Jones' farm, where Tabitha had met her husband. Now Tabitha had a friend, and all her other children were on Lord Osberton's lake. Then they came to Mr Giles' farm and Emma turned along the path by the wood so that she could see the field where the hens were now allowed to roam. A few were still out, scratching, but most had retired to the barn for the night. That was another good thing that had happened …

Emma turned back along the wide grass verge and

headed for home. She was hungry now and longed for the warm kitchen, and her mother's smiling face, and supper, with Solomon on the stove, and Bodger in his basket, and Nelson chattering from his aviary.

Suddenly she stopped dreaming. Freckles was quivering beneath her, his muscles were bunched and tense, his ears laid back.

There was a heavy road-roller standing in the road, and of all things Freckles hated road-rollers. He hated them even more than tractors.

"Freckles, stop! Freckles, behave!" she cried, as he shied and pranced and bucked and tried to bolt. At last she brought him under control, and he stood quiet, still tense, but on the other side of the steam roller.

Emma felt very pleased with herself. She had successfully got him round a steam roller, and she hadn't fallen off.

"They won't believe this at home," she told him. "You may trot now. I said trot, not canter. Freckles, I did not say gallop. Freckles, stop!"

They arrived home rather fast. She led him into the yard.

After supper Emma went outside. Freckles wasn't in the yard. With the help of a torch she found her way into the garden and discovered him in the orchard, feasting on fallen apples.

"Oh, Freckles," she scolded him, "You can't be left alone for five minutes without getting into mischief, can you?"

She picked up his halter and pulled him along behind her, past the pond beside which just two ducks were now sitting.

"Goodnight, Tabitha. Goodnight, friend," she called. "I'll give you a name tomorrow."

She bent down to pick up a large red apple which

Freckles hadn't noticed. He butted her from behind, so that she nearly fell over.

"I wish you wouldn't do that," she cried. "Why do I love you so much, when you behave so badly? And you've eaten everything on the bird table. There'll be trouble about that."

She led him through the yard into his paddock. He put his head on her shoulder and she stroked his nose.

"You may be a handful," she told him, "but I wouldn't change you for the whole world. Who wants a rocking horse, anyway?"